EMBERS OF MURDER

ALEC PECHE

ACKNOWLEDGMENTS

As a California resident, I watch the state catch on fire each summer and fall. I'm surprised when I hear stories about arson caused fires. I think the endless acres of dry brush offers unlimited opportunities for arsonists to be thrilled with the power of fire. I knew Jill Quint had to get involved with an arson case.

Many thanks to my first readers and especially GM Meyer and Ellen Falk. You turn my imagination into readable English with each story. Thank you for your brilliant editing.

CHAPTER 1

Amanda Moore parked her truck on a wide shoulder of the road that meandered through the low hills leading to Sequoia National Forest. Everywhere she looked, it was a dream landscape for her. She was an arsonist, and she viewed the endless dry brush around her, fantasizing about what the hillside would look like ablaze. She heard the crackling sounds of trees snapping. She felt the heat of the fire, and that was saying something as the warm August air was shaping up to be a one-hundred-degree day. The pull of the fire was so strong, she held her hands out to warm them in the flames. Then she blinked and pulled herself back to the present.

She had plans for this hillside. In a few days, she would meet her latest target here for a hike and a picnic. It was hard to hold off the urge to torch the hillside. She heard the whispers of the flames calling her. She had to pause and clear that vision from her mind. When she returned home, she would enjoy lighting her many candles so she could watch the power of fire dancing. First, though, she had to find the hiking trail.

Amanda walked a quarter mile up the road and found the trail she had read about. She followed the trail as it slowly crept uphill.

The hiker who mentioned this trail said about a half mile into the trail, it reached a plateau with a nice view of the surrounding area. They also said that the trail was deserted. They hiked it for solitude as they never met another hiker on the trail. This was perfect for her needs. She listened and thought she heard someone coming; she ducked behind a tree. She listened harder and then decided that it was just the wind. When she came back here with her target and started a brushfire, she would take a brief moment to chuckle with her friend the wind and enjoy the flames before she made her escape from the scene of the crime.

She walked the area a little more, looking for an alternative path back to her truck. This was her third fire this year. So far, she had managed to make them look like natural events. She studied the weather for red flag fire warning days. In any given year, the cause of about a third of state brushfires was labeled *undetermined,* and Amanda wanted to keep her fires in that category. The state of California arrested about seventy arsonists a year. Despite her history of setting over fifty fires, she hadn't been caught.

This time Amanda was trying something new. She had been on various dating sites looking for her ideal man. So far, she hadn't found him. Indeed, she found a lot of duds. Guys with whom a second date was out of the question in her mind. She decided some men just needed to be taken out of the dating pool. She would help her fellow females looking for mates by permanently eliminating some of the dating pool dregs.

Her next brushfire was going to include one of those dregs. There would be a red flag warning in three days according to the weather service, and she set up a second date with a man she hadn't liked on the first date. Everything in his profile was a stretch of the truth. He was three inches shorter, ten years older, and forty pounds heavier than his profile. And those were the nice things she could say about him. His name was Derek Henry, and the hike to the plateau would be his last. She hoped that he could make it as far as she needed him to walk, given his age and weight.

She promised a beautiful view and a great picnic lunch, and he would get to hit a home run afterward. That last promise locked him in.

Little did Derek know that he would be sound asleep before he could ever step up to bat. Amanda had shopped for sleeping pills from several doctors. She studied the dosage she needed to kill him as the brush caught fire around him. If she was successful in killing Derek, she planned to move on to helium gas. She was worried that if the authorities autopsied him, they would find the sleeping pills in his stomach. The fire experts would spend some time figuring out if Derek died by suicide, homicide, or merely an accident. She paused to review the murder scene in her head, trying to think of additional evidence she could leave that would make it look like an accidental death. She would have to leave a review of this hiking area in the future saying it was burned in a fire. It would take a couple of years, and then the brush would grow back.

The next man she planned to meet for a hike would be offered the opportunity for a little fun with inhaling helium. The high-pitched voice of helium would be entertainment. She would be sure to have her next victim inhale enough pure helium to render himself unconscious. Then she might blow some nitrogen gas over his face just to make sure he would die. Then, she'd start another fire, but this time there wouldn't be evidence of the sleeping drugs in his belly. She'd bet the coroner would think he died of natural causes. Was being a jerk a natural cause of death?

She laughed to herself as she finished exploring the area. Amanda checked her watch as she had to work that day if she wanted to pay the bills. She did freelance coding and abstracting of medical charts. She could work from the trailer she towed behind her truck and name her hours each day as long as she finished her work sometime within the twenty-four-hour period. Her trailer had a satellite dish, so she could always access the internet for her work. The trailer allowed her to move around the state at will. She had an hour drive back to her campsite and would spend the remainder of the day doing the work at her computer. It wasn't exciting, but that was what fire was for it was her exciting friend.

For her first date with Derek, she purposely arranged a meeting where alcohol was served to figure out his drinking habits and favorite libations. She planned to serve him his drink of choice during her picnic. Her sleeping pills would be crushed into his beverage, which had been a mojito on their first date. She spent the past few days experimenting with the mojito. She wanted to make sure that the pills' bitter taste was hidden by the mint, sugar, and lime juice. She tasted the concoction then spit it out as she didn't want to kill herself with the dose meant for him. She refined her recipe and found the perfect cooler backpack that would carry her cocktail, the mint, and ice cubes in separate containers that she would mix with a flourish to be served to Derek.

All that was left for her to do was wait a few days for their meeting. When she decided to go forth with this plan for removing the dregs from the dating pool, she debated whether to meet Derek at the start of the hiking site or for them to drive together into the hills. She decided on the first option, as the evidence of an empty car would lend credence to the thought that his death was an accident or suicide.

If he didn't show at the appointed time, she would walk away unfulfilled with a fire. She wouldn't start a brushfire in his absence as she might save this location for her next target. She would dump her sleeping pill cocktail and plan her next fire, but she really hoped that Derek would show up. She was itching to start a fire. Lighting many of her candles at home was an unsatisfactory experience in place of a brushfire and the fulfillment she expected to feel when he was removed from the dating pool.

Amanda also researched what would happen to Derek's body as the brushfire ignited around him. If the sleeping pills didn't kill him, he would die from smoke inhalation. His clothing might catch on fire, but his body wouldn't. It wasn't hot enough at the start of a fire to do more than burn his clothing. His face would still be identifiable, and his fingerprints would be available to authorities for comparison. After he fell asleep, she would check his pockets for a phone and wallet. She would make sure the phone was turned off, and there were no pictures or texts of hers saved on it. She would remove any cash but leave everything else intact in his wallet. There was no sense in wasting any cash he might have—far better for her to spend it.

A couple of days later, Amanda found herself pulling onto the highway shoulder that she had identified days ago. She was early as she wanted to make sure she had room to leave the easement without moving Derek's car. She grabbed her backpack and placed it at her feet as she leaned against the truck awaiting his arrival. Her excitement was palpable, and Derek would probably mistake it as enthusiasm for him. An hour from now, she would be driving through these hills to another road that would take her back to her home. She didn't want to take the road that firetrucks would be using to arrive at the scene as she would look like she was fleeing the fire, which of course she was.

Soon she could hear the car's approach though it wasn't in view yet as this was a winding road. She continued leaning casually against her truck, waiting to see if Derek the dreg was behind the wheel. She verified it was him and gave a small wave, and watched him park behind her vehicle.

He got out of the car and said, "This sure is in the middle of nowhere. Are you sure you want to hike? We could head back to my house and grab a beer."

Amanda thought, "Hell no, I've got a plan for you a big, beautiful bonfire." Instead, she said, "Hey, it's pretty here; wait until you see the views. It's only a half mile, and then I've got stuff for our picnic, including the ingredients for a mojito. Don't make me waste the effort. I've also got a soft blanket for other things later, but let's start the walk, and then we'll drink mojitos to slake our thirst."

Derek nodded and then seemed to look around for a path to start the hike.

"Follow me. The path is just a little bit up this road," she said, gesturing where the trailhead was located.

Though she didn't like Derek, she gave some thought as to what they could chat about on the way to the plateau. As he loved himself, she asked him questions about his favorite this and that. It seemed to keep his mind off the fact that he was breathing heavily and sweating the more they hiked. He paused at one point, seeming to ask himself if a promise of sex was worth the effort of the hike. So she gave her best come hither look and said, "We have about another five minutes of walking, and then I'll have a refreshing mojito in your hand. I even have ice cubes in my pack. I'd hate to drink alone if you decide that it's too far to walk."

That seemed to be enough motivation to keep him moving as she heard steps behind her. It was a little more than five minutes at the pace they were walking, but when she saw him flagging again, she pulled a blanket out of her pack, saying, "Isn't this a nice soft blanket? We won't have to lay on the hard ground."

Again, she heard his steps pick up behind her. She picked up her pace so she would have a few extra moments alone. She wanted time to spread the blanket and pull the contents out of her pack so she could get him drinking fast. Unfortunately, her concoction didn't work immediately. Still, she had used a rum with a greater than seventy-five percent alcohol by volume, hoping to accelerate his disorientation. She wanted him to relax on the blanket. She didn't want to immediately have to refuse his sexual overtures.

She quickly mixed the cocktail and held it out to him. "Here's your mojito. It's going to taste wonderful and refreshing after that walk."

He was panting as he accepted the glass she held out to him.

Derek sure was out of shape and yet he saw himself as a wildly attractive man. Go figure! She poured a second drink from another container for herself. It looked like a mojito, but there were no sedatives or rum in her version. She toasted her glass to his and was happy to see him taking large swallows of the drink.

"I hated that walk. We aren't doing this again for a date."

"Oh, that's too bad. I love it here. The air is fresh, and the scenery is beautiful. What would you rather be doing?"

Keep him talking, so the alcohol and drugs have time to work.

"We could have just met at the Three Rivers Tavern. It's not as far a drive, and you don't have to walk for fifteen minutes."

"But doesn't the mojito taste better after you generated so much thirst on that walk?"

"Babe, this is a good tasting mojito. You must have used the good rum as I can already feel the buzz of this drink."

Amanda felt like doing a little dance. Something—either the drugs or the alcohol—was making its way to his brain. If this kept up, she wouldn't have to fend off a single amorous pass. He was stretched out on the blanket while she sat on a rock within reach to top off his drink.

"Have you finished your drink? I can refill you."

"That sounds like a good idea. What do you have to eat?"

"I brought cookies, chips, and sandwiches. Which would you like to start with?"

"I'm feeling tired after that long walk. Why don't you give me a cookie as that doesn't take much effort to eat."

Great! Derek was starting to feel sleepy from the drink. That was the whole purpose of the drink and its unique ingredients. Before she fetched a cookie, she topped off his drink. Then she dug through her backpack to find the cookies. She had laced the chocolate chip cookies with marijuana so he would have quite a cocktail in his system. She needed him awake enough to finish the second glass just to ensure he had enough drugs on board to sleep through any fire that caught his clothing. Besides, she wanted to search him, and she didn't want him to wake up during her search.

She kept up her conversation and watched his eyelids get heavier.

"I'm sorry, Babe, but I need a nap," Derek said, just before he passed out.

Amanda made a grab for the drink before it tipped all over the blanket. She took a look at the contents, happy to see that most of the second glass was gone. Hurray, now all she needed to do was wait and hope she didn't have the bad luck of the occasional hiker appearing in this area. If that happened, she would have to assure the person that Derek was asleep because he worked a long shift, not because he was dead.

Amanda waited another ten minutes, then tried to shake Derek awake after she put gloves on. He barely moved his hand. So she began searching his pockets. She pulled his wallet out and found fifty dollars for her effort. She replaced the wallet in the back pocket. Next, she pulled out a cell phone from the side pocket of his cargo shorts. He didn't have a lock on his phone, so she went to his contacts and erased her name and the text messages they had exchanged. She debated erasing his entire phone, but that would be suspicious. She checked his pulse, and it was slow, and she could barely see his chest rising. He was on his way out. Perhaps another five minutes, and his heart would stop. She grabbed his car keys and started back to where the cars were parked, happy to see there were no hikers and no one else had parked in the little easement. She searched his car to be sure that there was no evidence connecting her, and she found none.

She made her way back to where he was lying on the blanket. He looked very pale, unmoving, and dead. She rolled him off the blanket, which she would destroy once she returned to civilization. She put an old cigarette butt close to his fingers, then sprinkled the ground around him with a bottle of isopropyl alcohol. Unlike gasoline, isopropyl alcohol would be harder to detect by investigators. She then did another check to make sure there were no hikers in the area, and she lit a match. The dry brush caught on fire, and she took off at a run for her truck. Ten minutes later, she could see smoke drifting toward the sky from the blaze even though she was some distance away. She'd been successful in leaving the area before the fire trucks arrived. She hadn't passed a single person or car on her return out of the hills. Now, she would wait and watch the news. It would be on television soon, and she was interested in hearing from fire experts on the cause of the fire.

CHAPTER 2

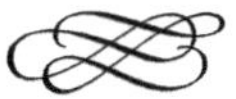

*J*ill Quint, MD, forensic pathologist, PI, and vintner, yawned as she watched her last barrel of newly harvested muscat grape juice forklifted into her wine cellar. It would rest there a year or two until she liked the taste of the wine and determined it was ready for bottling. So far, she nailed the perfect aging time as each of her vintages sold out. This was an exhausting time of the year with the physical labor of picking grapes in the hot sun. It was hard to drink enough water to keep up with her body's water loss through sweat. She also kept an eye on her workers, not wanting any of them to suffer from heatstroke. They started picking at sunrise and stopped around noon before the temperatures exceeded one-hundred degrees. It took less than a week to do her entire acreage, but these were intensive days for Jill. Her Dalmatian, Trixie, knew they wouldn't go for any runs the week of the harvest as even the dog was exhausted from being outside at Jill's side every day.

It was the end of a long week, and she planned nothing more than a celebratory glass of her first Moscato vintage and a pepperoni pizza with her partner, Nathan Conroy. She figured she would nod off by the third piece. He'd seen her through other

"

vintages and knew she had three things on her mind—pizza, wine, and sleep.

Just as she was entering her house to grab a shower, her cell phone rang, and oddly enough, it was from her old work number —the Sacramento Coroner's Office.

"Hello, this is Jill Quint."

"Hi Jill, it's Jennifer Galloway. Do you have a few minutes to talk?"

"For an old colleague, sure. What's up?" Jill asked, sitting down on her front stoop.

"You heard about the bus accident in the fog on Highway 99?"

"Yes," Jill replied, thinking surely they weren't asking her back to work for a few days on a mass casualty incident.

"All of our resources are taken up dealing with the fifty-six bus deaths. We've had another case reach our lab that could use your expertise."

Whew, thought Jill, she wouldn't have to think of an excuse to turn down her old colleague.

"We've had three single men found within brushfire areas in the past six weeks. We're wondering if they're connected. The most recent victim was sent here, as the county couldn't do the autopsy."

"Are you asking for my help as a PI or as a forensic pathologist?"

"Both, actually. That's what made me think of you. Would you be able to come to our office early tomorrow? You can review the evidence there and help us decide where to go next."

Jill thought about what perfect timing it was for this call. She had just finished a crucial part of her wine business, and at that very moment was free to move on to just about anything. On the other hand, she hated fire with a passion. It scared her how fast fire could destroy. The fact that her city was surrounded by dry brush each summer magnified that fear. She had never visited a fire scene while working for the state. They had wildfire victims come in, but she did her work in the autopsy suite and not in the field.

"I'll be there at eight. Does that work for you?" Jill replied.

"That's perfect and feel free to bring a bottle of your wine. I haven't been able to find it in a store in Sacramento."

"Do you like Moscato wine?"

"Do the leaves turn brown every fall? Of course I like Moscato!"

"Okay, I'll come with a bottle in hand."

"You're the best, Jill!"

They ended their call and Jill spent a few moments thinking about the case potential. Lone men were found dead in brushfire areas. It happened every year that she could recall while working for the state. The men were always homeless or antisocial hermits. They often started the fire that killed them, and usually it was due to a cigarette or unattended campfire. She began sweating even more as she saw herself in her imagination being surrounded by fire, unable to breathe, and knowing that a painful death awaited her. As if sensing her distress, Trixie leaned in and licked her face, which snapped her out of her scary visions. She gave the dog a hug for always seeming to know what she needed.

She stood up to walk into her house, relieved that it was cooler inside. She debated heading upstairs to shower or walk over to her computer and do a Google search of recently announced deaths connected to wildfires. She decided it could wait as her brain could do with a rest from the sun and heat over the past few days. So, she headed upstairs to her shower. She had enough time to clean up, and then she would load her car for the drive north early the next morning.

Once she was clean and presentable, she loaded her autopsy kit and laptop into her car. It was a two-hour drive to her old office, and she wanted to get moving early the next morning. She was zoning out on her sofa watching a home decorating show on television. Her feet rested on her coffee table, and her glass of

Moscato was in her hand. She heard Nathan tap and open her front door carrying her beloved pizza.

"You look relaxed, happy, and sleepy, all at once," Nathan said, leaning down to kiss her as he set the pizza box on the coffee table.

Jill thought a moment about the adjectives he used to describe her current mood and decided she agreed with them.

"I am all of those descriptions. I'm relaxed because of the wine and the television show, happy that my harvest is done, and sleepy from several days of hard work. How was your day?"

"Let me grab some plates and a glass of wine, and I'll tell you about my latest project," Nathan said, walking into her kitchen to do just that.

He sat down next to her with the requisite supplies, and they spent a few moments digging into their respective slices of pizza. Jill's half was pepperoni, ham, olives, and pineapple, while Nathan liked everything on his side of the pie.

"So what's up?" Jill asked, once her initial hunger was assuaged.

"You can call me Professor."

"Really? Professor of what?"

"My alma mater has hired me to teach wine marketing. I'll be teaching the next generation of label makers and brochure designers whose purpose is to promote wine."

"I didn't know you wanted to do that. Congrats on your new title," Jill said, leaning in to kiss him.

"Frankly, I didn't know I wanted to do that either. Do you remember a couple of months ago when I gave a guest lecture at the university? Apparently, the school got rave reviews and reached out to see if I could teach more."

"That's great, Sweetie! Will you drive there once a week or something like that? It's about ninety minutes or so if you avoid rush hour."

"Actually, I'll stay overnight as they'll have me teaching—two classes one on brand management and one on digital design. I'll also have office hours on those two days."

"Wow. That's so cool! The students will be lucky to have you," Jill said.

"Thanks. I enjoy teaching, and I think I have enough of a portfolio that I'm qualified to give expert advice. Someday I may take on a partner, but in the near term, I can offer students internships at my company, which will help me and help them."

"Wow. I'm so impressed. Why didn't you say anything before now about this dream to teach?"

"There was no point in talking about it until I knew it could come to fruition. My alma mater is the only school where I wanted teach. I don't have a doctorate or even a Master's degree, so I thought I'd never gain footing in the academic world."

"Yeah, but you're so brilliant at what you do. Yours is an ever-changing field reflecting consumer taste. The fact that you've led the way on brilliant designs counts for those who follow you. Let's toast."

"I thought we were supposed to be toasting to the completion of your harvest."

"My harvest happens once a year. Your announcement is a once in a lifetime accomplishment. Cheers to you," she said, clinking his glass.

"At least you get to sleep in tomorrow after all the physical labor of the past few days," Nathan said.

"Actually, I don't. I need to be on the road to my former office in Sacramento. I've been asked to look into a suspicious death in a wildfire."

"Why? They've never called before for your help, have they?" Nathan said, trying to remember the various groups of people that Jill had worked with. Then Nathan was reminded of one of Jill's phobias. "Will you be okay dealing with fire victims?"

"Do you remember the bus crash on Interstate 99 yesterday? I guess they're fully occupied with the victims. They have another case that requires a little forensic pathology and a little private investigator work, so they thought to call me. I need to be there at eight. As for the fire part of these investigations, I don't know how I'll handle that. Wish me luck."

"I do wish you luck, but I bet your biggest fear is they'll change their minds and call you off the case." Nathan said with a smile knowing how Jill's brain worked.

"Exactly. I'm pleased my former office thought of me, and I don't have anything that has to be completed tomorrow. Sure, there's stuff to do around this winery, but it can wait a day while I go play sleuth."

"Okay, that's another thing to toast to. I'd grab a ride with you, as I need to stop by the university, but you might be gone all day, and I'd get stuck waiting for you to return. Besides, you're probably leaving at six, which is way too early for me to head out. Maybe in the future, we can coordinate our drives. So what's the case?"

"I don't have many details, and I was tempted to Google my questions, but instead, I decided to wait until I get to Sacramento."

"Why do they want you to sleuth?" Nathan asked as he hadn't ever seen Jill agree to work a case with so little information about the victim.

"They have found three men by themselves in three wildfires across the state. I think they want me to determine if there's any connection."

"Aren't they likely connected?"

"Not necessarily. You would be surprised by the number of homeless or what I'll call hermit men, who eventually die in a wildfire. Often, they drink and smoke while near a lot of tinder. If you've been living on the streets awhile, your health may not be the best, and you may move too slow to avoid a fire. They also start fires to stay warm, and sparks from the fire can quickly become a brushfire."

"So, what do you have to examine? Is it just a burnt-out corpse?" Nathan asked with both curiosity and revulsion.

"Actually, we humans don't burn very well as we're too full of water. A crematory will reduce you to ashes at over fourteen-hundred degrees. Most brushfires don't get close to that temperature. Back to your question, the clothes may burn off, and there may be a few second-degree burns on the face, and the hair will likely burn off. The face should be identifiable, and fingerprints are usually intact. Victims don't die from the fire; they die from smoke inhalation or super-heated air. A forest fire can get as hot as a crematory after it has picked up the dry brush and become larger, but it wouldn't be that hot at the start of the fire, which should be where the victim is found."

"You have a brain full of weird information. I think that for most humans, dying by being burned alive is a terrifying thought. Isn't that the source of your fear about fire?"

"It is, but unless you're tied at the stake on top of a bonfire, the smoke will render you unconscious before you feel the heat of the fire. Let's go back to discussing your new job; our thoughts are too gruesome on an otherwise excellent evening."

CHAPTER 3

*A*s planned, Jill found herself pulling into the parking lot of her former employer right on schedule. She could see the lot was almost full and knew her ex-colleagues were working around the clock to collect evidence from the remains of the bus crash victims. These had an added layer of being a tour group visiting from a foreign country, so there was more paperwork to move the bodies home. Rather than having a badge to get her inside, she stopped and talked to an intercom outside the door to the building, and soon she was buzzed inside.

She approached the desk where an assistant sat whom she recognized from her days on the job.

"Nice to see you this morning, Dr. Quint. I was notified that you were coming. Let me get Dr. Galloway here to escort you."

A door opened on the far side of the lobby, and out came Jennifer Galloway.

The assistant smiled and said, "I was just about to buzz you."

"I remember from my time working with Dr. Quint that she was a stickler for being on time, and I can see you haven't changed," Jennifer said, holding out her hand to shake Jill's.

"Sorry, I can't help myself. It's my little bit of OCD. I must be on time."

Jennifer escorted Jill behind the locked door. She paused to say, "I'm grateful as we're overloaded right now and appreciate your help. I have permission to hire you for this case as a per diem if that's okay with you. We budgeted up to eighty hours of your time. Just submit timesheets to me, and we'll get you paid. Is that good?"

"Yes. I wasn't sure I was getting paid. You asked for my help and I came."

"I'm just glad you were available."

"Actually, your timing was exquisite. I had just finished putting my grape harvest into barrels for aging about an hour before you called. If you had called the day before, I would have been unavailable as the grapes are time-sensitive. Speaking of which, here's your bottle of Moscato," Jill said, pulling the bottle out of her backpack.

"You have such a glamorous life. You're a PI, and you harvest grapes and make my favorite wine. Can I live your life?"

Jill laughed and said, "Someday, yes. Dare I tell you I also have the perfect partner and a wonderful dog? However, when you called, I was sitting in the heat with broken fingernails, sweat matted hair, and dirt and dust all over me. I was trying to find the energy to climb my stairs to take a shower."

Jennifer laughed and said, "I miss you here in the crime lab. No matter how tense the situation, you could always find something to make us laugh or feel good about our work."

"So tell me what you need help with."

"We have three men reportedly dying at wildfire scenes about two weeks apart. Each man was found after a wildfire was extinguished. Apparently, the fire personnel walk through the burn area to ensure there are no remains left behind. Each man has been found within a burn zone. Each man had a mobile phone and a wallet on their person. They died from smoke inhalation in all three cases, though the first man also had benzodiazepines on board. All three men were in their thirties or forties, had drunk alcohol just before their death. None appeared to be homeless or own land in the immediate area around the wildfire."

"So the victims are all a little too similar for their deaths to appear to be accidental, but you have no evidence of homicide. They had alcohol on board, but probably not enough to make them unaware of the fire. You want me to find out if they're linked."

"Exactly!"

"I can do that. Did you call the neighboring states to see if they had any similar cases?"

"I didn't, and that's a good idea. It might help confirm if this is just the law of the averages or something really sinister."

"Are all three victims here?" Jill asked.

"No, but all the forensic evidence is. The latest victim is here, but the other two were processed through Kern and Fresno counties. I believe the remains were already released as the oldest case is about four weeks old. We wouldn't have noticed the connection among the three cases except that an insurance adjuster named Jack called us up to say that this was the third male victim he knew of in the fires he inspected for insurance claims. He worked the insurance claims for all three. He was the only common factor among different fire departments, cops, and medical examiners."

"Could he be a suspect?"

"I hadn't thought of that, and that's why we need your special skills here. I've got a computer for you to look at the results. You're welcome to examine the latest victim as he's in our storage. We're still processing the bus accident. The autopsy room is full, so I've arranged a computer in our conference room. You can call me to let me know if you need to examine our latest victim once you work your way through the evidence. Sound like a plan?"

"Sounds perfect. I left my autopsy kit out in the car, but I brought my forms that I use to track other cases, so I should be able to provide you with a report of my findings. I'm going to call Oregon and Washington to see if they have had any fire victims. Do I have your permission to say I represent this office?"

"Of course. You may already know those people up north from your time here."

"I don't remember contacting them about any case, but I'll admit my brain thinks differently now that I don't have to focus on completing all of the right paperwork."

"Again, can I have your life?" Jennifer asked, and when Jill shook her head no with a smile, she added, "We have lunch being delivered. I'll notify you when it arrives if you want to join us."

"I'd love to, thanks."

They arrived at the conference room, entered the room, and approached the computer. Jill followed the instructions for access, and soon she was bringing up the files related to the case. Jennifer nodded and left to return to her crew in the autopsy room.

Jill settled in to read the materials in front of her and think about these cases. After the first pass, she looked up the names of who she thought might be responsible in Oregon and Washington for similar incident reports and made a few calls. She came up empty-handed as no one could remember a single man dying suspiciously in any brush fire. A search of the database verified this. She was about to check all counties in California when she got a text about lunch. It was laid out in a break room that Jill remembered well. She was reacquainted with the staff she had worked with and met new members of the team. They asked about her new life, and she caught up with theirs. Soon it was time to get back to work. Mostly she was holding her fears and nightmares about the dangers of fire at bay.

She sent off messages to the other counties to see if they had had a recent case of lone men dying in their wildfires. Wildfire season occurred every year in California as there was no rain from May to November. During that time, anything that didn't have a water supply dried out and became ignitable tinder. There were just under eight thousand wildfires in the prior year, and if there were deaths, they seem to be concentrated in a particular fire. So lone male victims should be easy to find. While she was waiting for a reply, she went back to a second pass at the forensic records.

The men were clothed and had wallets with IDs and credit cards, but no cash. They also had phones on them that were returned to the families. All were single, Caucasian, and between a relatively narrow age range. All were employed and left their cars in the area. They appeared to be there for a hike. About a mile into the hike, they stopped for a drink and a smoke. They fell asleep and their lit cigarette started a wildfire.

Jill agreed with the fire insurance inspector. This all seemed contrived and convenient. Jill couldn't think of a single person she knew who liked to hike but was also a smoker. Then she paused and realized she didn't have any friends who smoked, so that was a faulty conclusion. She wondered if the autopsy showed cigarette damage to the lungs or throat? She pulled out the three sets of paperwork on her victims. The narrative mentioned damage from smoke inhalation, but that was from the fire. The cigarette found near the body was identified as a famous brand. It wasn't an herbal nicotine-free cigarette. If her hiker was a smoker, he should have nicotine in his blood and hair. She could sample the current victim here to see if he was. If his blood came back nicotine-free, then the death became suspicious. If his blood came back with nicotine, he was a smoker or had been exposed to secondhand smoke.

Jill left the conference room to search in the specimen room for the container of the victim's blood. She texted Jennifer before she did so in case she had concerns, but she was okay with Jill's access. She used a cotinine test device in the lateral flow chromatographic immunoassay to test the victim's blood. Cotinine was the break-down of nicotine in the blood. Brushfires didn't contain nicotine, so she didn't have to worry about a false positive. Minutes later, she had her answer. There was no cotinine in the victim's blood, so the cigarette was either a prop left by the murderer or left by someone else. Again, she found it hard to believe, the butt would have been left by another hiker, close to where their murder victim decided to rest. Who looks around for a place to rest while hiking and purposely chooses to sit or lay down next to an old cigarette butt? This was very suspicious. The butt had been sent off for DNA analysis, but they were back-logged, and it was routine, not a high priority case, so they wouldn't get the results back for months.

She retrieved the records from the other victims to see if they also had butts near the body. There was no mention of butts found at either crime scene. She wondered if it was there but hadn't been recovered. Maybe she would take a ride to the three murder scenes tomorrow. She'd take Trixie with her as her nose was good at smelling things. Of course, if the fire scene was the stuff of her nightmares, the dog might also help her out emotionally.

If she had the dog sniff a cigarette, she would then go find it at the scene. It wouldn't even have to be the same brand. The scenes were hundreds of miles apart, so she would visit the two oldest sites to the south first. She wrote down the coordinates of the murder scenes to know where to drive the next day. She located Jennifer just before she left for the day.

"So, what did you think? Is the insurance investigator on to something?"

"Perhaps. The victim in your cooler was not a smoker. I did a cotinine test on his blood. So who left the cigarette there? I know you sent it out for DNA analysis, but the results won't be back for a few months, probably. How many hikers do you know who are also smokers?"

Jennifer thought for a moment and then replied, "None."

"Exactly. Where did the cigarette come from, then? Why was the scene of death made to look like he fell asleep after smoking?"

"Those are excellent points that we should have thought to evaluate."

"No, the detective or whoever was working the death should have asked you to run the test. Your job was to establish the cause of death, and you did."

"You're right, but I must say that playing both the forensic person and the detective looks like fun."

"I'll admit that I like getting justice for our victims. Justice is why I provide second opinions on the cause of death. It's a step beyond just figuring out what killed someone. The *who* part of the equation is fun also."

"Okay, I'll hold our victim's remains another two days before releasing them to the family in case you come up with a clue from one of the other death sites that needs to be researched with our current victim."

"Thanks. I'll see you in a few days. Good luck with your bus crash victims."

"Thanks, Jill. It's been good to have you around. You stimulate my tired brain."

CHAPTER 4

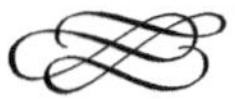

Jill was on her way to a small remote area northeast of Bakersfield. Trixie was asleep in the back. They had been on the road for about an hour after she stopped to buy a pack of cigarettes. She never felt such revulsion over a purchase, but she needed something for Trixie to smell. She didn't dare pick up a cigarette butt off the ground, given the germs it might carry and the confusing scents that might be on the butt. She bought the same brand as the butt found at the scene of their third victim, although this was the site of the first victim. She followed her GPS to the coordinates of where the body was located. She came upon a fire zone and stopped her car, not sure she wanted to go forward. What if the fire reignited and she was trapped? The fire had been out for several weeks, but she couldn't let go of the idea that something else in the desolate landscape could burn.

She needed to get a grip on her imagination.

She started looking for an appropriate place on the road to park. She could smell the fire. Jill had an excellent nose for detecting fire as she was so scared and paranoid about it. It was good the fire was extinguished so she could inspect the scene where the first victim was found. Some wildfires took weeks to be put out. There had been a fire in a remote area of Yosemite that raged for over three months.

She pulled over when she saw a wide shoulder in the road. She put Trixie on her leash, and grabbed a water bowl and jug, an evidence kit, and the cigarettes. She walked around looking for a trail, then she decided that was a waste of time. The fire completely changed the landscape and there were no trails. She listened for a while but heard no sounds of a fire, and she could see no smoke, so she relaxed. There was no dead brush to walk through either, so it was a matter of pulling out her compass to find the coordinates of where the victim was found. Besides Trixie's excellent work as a scent hound, she was glad for the large dog as visiting a fire scene was quite creepy.

Without the leaves rustling, she could hear the trees groaning. Thankfully, there wasn't any fog, or she would be looking for zombies to chase her out of the trees, or rather what was left of the trees. They were mostly upright blackened sticks. She would have to look up whether dogs held zombies off, or would she need to jog away, making sure the dog kept pace with her. Hopefully, the fire personnel who cleared the fire scene left no undead to rise up as zombies. Isn't that what made a zombie? She shook her head at her weird thoughts and continued to follow the compass to her spot. It was better to worry about zombies than be paralyzed by a fire scene. She arrived on a plateau then paced off a circle of the geocoordinates as they weren't exact. It was more like a forty-foot circle.

She stepped outside of the circle and put the dog's water bowl down, and filled it. After Trixie drank her fill, Jill held out a cigarette from the purchased pack and said to the dog, "Find."

She guided the dog around where she thought the rough circle was, and as she was coming to an end of the search, Trixie focused on a spot. Jill put on latex gloves and knelt to gently clear the debris away with a screwdriver. The ground was covered in black debris, making it hard to see stuff. She saw the shape of a butt and used tweezers to drop it into a baggie. She spent more time in the immediate area where Trixie located the butt, but she didn't find anything more to collect.

Out of her back pocket, she pulled out the folded papers containing the report on the overall fire and the report of the specific personnel who found the victim. Was there anything else she needed to look at here? She wasn't an expert on the properties of a wildfire, but the thought was the fire started in this area and then spread out from there to the full fire size of three-hundred acres. The victim would have been engulfed in smoke and flames early in the fire before it picked up speed and fuel, so his body hadn't had much in the way of burn damage. Still, she shivered at the thought of being burned by the flames.

Jill reread the reports one more time but couldn't think of anything else to examine at the brushfire site and the location where victim number one was found. She and Trixie headed back to her car. It was on to location number two, an hour's drive with a pit stop on the way for lunch and a bathroom. Jill again wanted to have Trixie sniff out the blackened land looking for any evidence.

As she pulled up to the second location, the first thing that hit her was how similar both scenes were. They were low foothills on deserted roads. The only parking spots were wide margins on a two-lane road, and there was no traffic and no people in the vicinity. Of course, who would choose to hike in a burnt-out area? The smell was not one of fresh air. The view was one of devastation, and it was depressing, which was the exact opposite of what you were hoping to see on a hike.

Again, Jill watched her coordinates and parked at the closest wide margin of the two-lane road. She had clean gloves, tweezers, and a screwdriver, but everything else in her pockets was the same as her visit to the first fire scene. She did a three-hundred-sixty degree review of her surroundings to ensure no smoke and no zombies. The area was clear, from what she could see.

Like the last scene, she had to hike about a mile from where she parked to where the victim had been found. She was starting to agree with the fire insurance adjuster that there were many similarities among these victims. It really helped her to visit the scenes despite her anxieties about fire. It was hard to ignore that while these geocoordinates were about sixty miles apart, the land-scape and the setup looked remarkably similar.

This time the geocoordinates represented a small flat area. To her surprise, she could hear flowing water close by. Was it a waterfall? Before examining the scene where the victim had been found, Jill's curiosity was killing her to find the source of the water sound. This was such a dry part of the state that she was surprised to hear the gurgling of water. She thought about letting Trixie drink from the small creek she found. She tied her up out of reach while she made sure the water was clean and not filled with ash from the fire. There was evidence of fire on both sides of the creek, so it wasn't a wide enough barrier to stop the spread of the flames. She gathered up water in her hands, and it looked clear. The fire had been extinguished over a week ago, so the ash was probably long gone. She untied Trixie and brought her over to the creek. The dog sniffed at the water and decided not to drink. You could lead a horse to water, but you couldn't make it drink. Oh well.

She returned to the area where the second victim was found. She again went through the routine of having Trixie smell a cigarette and then search for it in the area. It took the dog a little longer this time to find a cigarette butt. Still, she focused on an area, and Jill got out her tools and evidence bag, finding the requisite butt under the black soot of the wildfire. She wasn't sure that the butts would lead anywhere, but the evidence was evidence, and she would be a fool not to collect it.

She was walking back to her car when her phone came back

into contact with the cell towers. She noted she had a message from the insurance adjuster, Jack. She'd sent him an email asking questions about the fire. Then she mentioned she was visiting the two southern sites today, and he was welcome to meet her. He didn't have time to meet her at the first location, but he was currently parked behind what he presumed was her car. After replying to his email, she picked up her pace to meet him at the car.

She'd asked Jennifer if Jack could be their suspect if the deaths were ruled homicide and not accidental. She had gone a step farther and researched what she could of Jack's background and was satisfied that he wasn't their suspect since a social media post of his showed him to be a thousand miles away at the time of the first fire death.

She crossed the street to the two cars and saw the man whose picture matched that of Jack, the insurance inspector. He was a tall man of Scandinavian descent and a few years older than her.

"Hi, I'm Dr. Jill Quint, and this is Trixie."

They shook hands while he held out his other hand for the dog to sniff.

"Hi, I'm Jack with the Forest Insurance Company. I wasn't sure my telephone call to the state crime lab would go anywhere. I'm glad to see that someone is following up on my information."

"I'm not sure anyone else would have made the connection among these fire victims as they seem like one-offs in different jurisdictions. You were the only commonality among the victims, so thanks for making the call. Some things don't add up, but I'd be the first to admit that I'm not sure anyone would've looked for additional evidence in these cases."

"What did you find that didn't make sense?" Jack asked.

"With the third victim, crime scene staff collected a cigarette butt. The speculation by the fire marshal was that the victim fell asleep smoking and started a brush fire. However, he appears to be a man who was hiking in the area and not someone who was living outdoors in the wildfire area. I don't know about you, but personally, I don't know anyone who is a smoker *and* a hiker. The two qualities just don't go together. So, I ran additional tests on the third victim, and he was not a smoker. There is no evidence in his blood of the product that nicotine breaks down into."

"Were there cigarettes at each location where the dead men were found?"

"A cigarette butt was found in the third wildfire scene. Trixie is a sniffing dog, and I bought the brand of cigarettes found at the third scene and had her search the other two scenes for any cigarettes, and she found one at each scene. The first cigarette was sent in for DNA analysis, but it will be months coming back. I collected the two butts that Trixie found today, but it remains to be seen if these are evidence that will help solve the case. Certainly, it does make the three scenes appear to be connected. What are the odds that a man who smokes also hikes the great outdoors? What are the odds that all three men fell asleep and caused brushfires with their cigarette which wasn't extinguished before they fell asleep? What are the odds that all three cigarettes are the same brand? I don't have an answer to that last question, but I will soon. I'm trying to retrieve blood samples from the first two victims to run the blood for a nicotine test. The evidence is piling up that these are not accidental deaths."

"Of the brushfires I've inspected over the years, there have been a few that were started by someone throwing a cigarette butt out a window of a moving car. There have been other brushfires started by men camping in the area and losing control of a campfire. Either they threw something on the fire that caused sparks to fly everywhere, or they were not paying attention and did not clear the brush from a perimeter around the fire. That said, none of those men died during the fire. They tried to put it out, and when that didn't work, they ran to safety. Some of those men are in jail at the moment."

"How many fire scenes have you been to?" Jill asked.

"I've been to twenty to thirty brushfire scenes for insurance purposes. I've been to a lot more houses that were accidentally set on fire by Christmas trees or electrical wiring or for some other reason."

Jill looked at her watch and decided she had time to explore the scene more.

"I'd love to use your expertise; would you mind coming back to the scene with me and tell me how the fire occurred? It helps to have a vision in my head."

As they walked back to the area where the fire started, Jill quizzed him about unusual fires he'd seen in his professional career. In her career of providing second opinions on the cause of death, she so far had not had any fire victims. She also had no proof of an arsonist at work in these cases either. Instead, there were too many coincidences not to think that there was a human hand behind the three murders and brushfires.

"Where did your dog find the cigarette butt?" Jack asked.

Jill walked over to the spot and pointed, "Here."

"Fire likes to move uphill and likes to be pushed by the wind. Did the fire agency report mention the direction the wind was blowing at the time the fire started?"

Jill pulled out the report and opened it up to look. Jack, who had more experience looking at the reports, skimmed down and pointed to the weather comments. The report contained the approximate ambient temperature and humidity at the start of the fire and the wind direction. Of course, big fires could create their own weather, including bending the direction of the wind. This fire was contained at about a hundred acres, which would be considered small.

"So your victim, in theory, was lying close to the cigarette butt, and the wind was blowing in a southeast direction. If this is a case of arson, then he would've started the fire about here," Jack said, pointing to the ground. "And then the wind would've pushed the flames over the body."

"He?"

"I've not investigated a case of arson where the perpetrator wasn't a male, but I suppose it could've been a female. I think they are a much smaller segment of the arson population."

"I saw the autopsy pictures of the victim found at the site. The burns that he had were from a backpack that had nylon straps. His clothing otherwise didn't burn that well which makes me think that has something to do with where his body was in relation to the start of the fire. Wouldn't the fire have been at a much cooler temperature than when it picked up speed and fuel after it had been burning for a while?"

"Fire temperatures can get very hot very quickly with sufficient fuel, but I agree with you. Looking at the surrounding area and the trees closest to where you found your cigarette butt, the fire was not as intense here as it was close to where we parked on the road. There's a tree here that doesn't look particularly damaged, but down by the road, the trees are blackened sticks, which suggests the fire was more ferocious there."

"I read in the report that this fire is labeled with a cause of *undetermined*. Since the cigarette butt was here, that suggests to me that the fire personnel either didn't see it or didn't think it was the cause of this fire. What's your guess about that conclusion?"

"I generally find the fire personnel to be very thorough in looking for the cause of the fire. Certainly, if there's an arsonist on the loose, they want to bring law enforcement in to assist with apprehension. They also have sniffer dogs like your Trixie here, but we're in peak fire season, and maybe the dog wasn't available for the smaller fire. Also, maybe he couldn't see the butt if the body was covering it up."

"If the arsonist had used gasoline or, say, charcoal fluid to start the fire, the fire experts would have seen that, correct?"

"I'm not a fire expert, but in my observation, the fire would have had different properties if someone had doused the area with gasoline. Usually, you can smell it even after the fire has been put out."

"So if they detected gasoline anywhere close to this fire, it would be in the report?" Jill asked.

"Yes, and there would've been a definitive statement as to whether the gasoline started the fire or was in the path of the fire."

"I can't think of any additional questions for you. Is there something I should've asked you about this fire scene?"

"You've now seen two of the three locations that I visited. Did you see any similarities between these first two sites?"

"When I pulled into the parking space here, I was struck by how similar the two locations were. They were both located on a quiet two-lane road. These are low foothills, and there's plenty of dry brush. The difference between the two locations was the first one had a view of the surrounding hills and valleys. In contrast, this location has a babbling brook nearby, so they both had something to see at the end of the hike. I guess I should get a hiking guide for these areas to see if they're recognized hiking locations."

"I don't recall hearing water the first time I was here. However, there were other people making noise. Did you visit the water source?"

"I did. There's fire on both sides of the little creek, but the water is clear. I tried to get Trixie to drink it, but she passed on the experience of freshwater."

"You can lead a dog to water, but you can't make it drink."

"Yep," Jill replied, leaning over slightly to rub the dog's ears.

They began walking back to the cars when Jack added, "That was a good conclusion about something special being available at the end of the hike. Maybe these cases have something to do with hikers."

"Maybe."

They wrapped up the conversation, and Jill promised to stay in touch if she discovered any additional sites. Talking to Jack had been very helpful.

CHAPTER 5

$\mathcal{J}$ill thought about the idea that these murders were related to hiking. On the long drive home, she tried using her phone's verbal search commands to see if she could find hiking trails close to the two fires. She soon gave up as she couldn't be specific enough to get an intelligent answer to her search out of her phone.

She returned home and debated what to do with the cigarette butts. They were potentially forensic evidence, but could she process anything in her lab that might yield new information? Her lab, out in a barn on her property, did not do DNA analysis. She could do other analysis. Her lab was built for chemistry and toxicology.

She decided she would take one of the new cigarettes she purchased and do a side-by-side analysis of it versus the cigarette butt she collected at the second scene. Maybe that would yield some new information. First, she went into the house to take a shower. Even though it had been almost two hours since she was at the scene of a fire, she could smell soot on herself. While her fear of fire had been dialed back, just the smell of her clothing was enough to remind her of how much she was scared by fire. She stripped down to her undies just inside her front door and threw the clothing and shoes outside on the porch. She would clean those later before bringing them inside the house.

An hour later, the only soot she smelled was when she opened the bag containing the cigarette butt. Maybe all cigarette butts smelled this way? She didn't have enough experience with cigarettes to know. She was old enough to remember the smell of cigarettes in a crowded bar. Still, the smell of an active burning cigarette was different from a butt that had been sitting around in a fire zone. Indeed, there should be some water on it from the firefighters and potentially some of the red stuff that she had seen in places around the fire zone. She did a quick search to see what the stuff was and found it was red-dyed fire retardant to prevent the spread of fire by covering brush with a gooey flame-retardant substance. It was a mixture of iron oxide and ammonium phosphate. The iron oxide gave it the red color so that pilots could see from the air where they needed to drop the mixture to prevent the spread of the fire.

She put the two cigarettes in her analyzer. As she expected, they came back with the same result—tobacco, nicotine, tar, acetone, with a little ammonia and arsenic thrown in for good measure. Why would anyone inhale such a toxic group of chemicals? The clean, unsmoked cigarette had less carbon in it as it lacked the soot of the butt found at the fire scene. The cigarette butt contained something else not found on the original cigarette —isopropyl alcohol. That made no sense. Isopropyl alcohol was not in the flame-retardant materials sprayed by the airplanes. It was also highly flammable. A smoker wouldn't soak a cigarette in isopropyl alcohol to smoke it unless they wanted their face to catch on fire. She would reach out to the fire scene investigator and ask why someone would use isopropyl alcohol in a wildfire area. She remembered this victim had the remains of the backpack near him, but there was no mention of a bottle of isopropyl alcohol being located inside the backpack. As flammable as it was, it would incinerate a backpack. The victim's backpack was burned but not incinerated.

The difference in the cigarette composition was the only thing she found at the scene besides acknowledging that both wildfire areas had something to see at the end of the hike. The first scene had the view. And the second scene had that creek with the beautiful sounds it made. It was time to move on to determining if both locations were designated as hiking sites. That might help her understand why the victims had been found where they were. Of course, if there was an arsonist behind these deaths, there were so many hiking trails throughout California that it would not be a useful fact to aid in predicting where the arsonist would strike next.

She checked the temporary mailbox she had with the Sacramento Coroner's Office to see if any other counties had responded to her inquiry about deaths in local wildfires. There were fifty-eight counties in California, and she knew of three counties with suspicious deaths. That left fifty-five counties for her to hear from. Looking at her inbox, she had perhaps forty responses, which was surprisingly good. Some of the counties were small, and the person receiving the email would likely have to refer to someone else to answer. She started opening the emails one by one, and by the time she got to the twentieth email, no county could find a report of a lone male who died in a wildfire this fire season. She kept going and found no other positive responses. So that appeared to be a dead end.

Jill moved on to looking at the locations where the bodies had been found. She researched online what hikers said about the hike through the fire area. There was a known trail in each case. It was hiked enough to flatten the brush, but the hikers who reviewed the trails mentioned that they never saw another person while on the hike. They appeared not to be well-traveled hiking trails. What could she do with that piece of information? Was she any closer to determining if this was an accidental death or a homicide? The answer was that she had more information, but it wasn't conclusive. If she had been the medical examiner for these victims, she didn't have enough evidence to rule their deaths as deliberate. That said, there sure were a lot of commonalities about the locations where the bodies were found.

So what was her next step? How could she help her former employer reach a conclusion about the three victims? As much as she hated to think it, she needed another victim with live evidence for her to review. She looked at the schedule of how far apart the victims died. Each one was two weeks to the day of the previous one. That meant that if they had a serial arsonist, he or she would kill someone else in less than a week based on the date of the past death. She put her thoughts into an email to Jennifer to update her on her progress with the case. The bottom line for Jill was that she was convinced there was an arsonist at work here, given the strange similarities among all these cases. She had no proof, but she noted that if there was a serial arsonist at work, the next murder would be in five days. Rather than use up the eighty hours of her contract immediately, she planned to visit the third site the next day and then lay off the case for a few days to see if there was an additional death. It wasn't a great strategy, but it was all she had at the moment.

Jill finished up at the lab and checked in with Nathan to see if he was available for dinner that night. He was, and they would meet at his house, and he would cook. What more could a girl ask for? A wonderful man and intelligent partner, flexible, a great cook with a fabulous wine cellar. The only rub was that Arthur, Nathan's cat, and Trixie hated each other's guts. For Jill and Nathan, the two animals provided much amusement.

The next morning, on her way to the third and most recent wildfire, Jill made a slight detour to Nathan's new employer, the university, to drop off his signed contract. They had had a lovely evening together and she was smiling as she remembered their first goodnight kiss so long ago.

When Jill and Trixie reached the third site, the burnt smell was much more pungent as the fire had been more recent and larger than the two wildfire locations she visited the previous day. After she exited her car, she leaned against it, listening for the sounds of fire but heard nothing. The fire must indeed be out. As she already had a cigarette butt from this site, she did not have Trixie search for one. Again, she was struck by how similar this third site was to the first two locations. She just needed to figure out what the drawing point of this site was. She didn't hear a babbling brook, nor did the trail have a beautiful view. When she returned home, she would research this area to see what hikers said about the trail that she had somehow missed in her visit today.

Who might be the serial arsonist? Why was that person targeting men in their thirties and forties? How were they starting the fires? Why weren't the men running from the fire? Usually, you don't allow yourself to be burnt at the stake, so to speak, without trying to run away. Certainly, that was Jill's nightmare. Yet, the second two victims appeared to have nothing in their system that would've stopped them from running away from the fire.

Jill pulled out the autopsy report of the victim from this site. He had minimal burns. Then she thought of something. What had the victim actually died from? He had hardly any evidence of smoke inhalation in his lungs, and she didn't recall that there was evidence of a lot of soot in the victim's throat and lungs. She looked through the paperwork for the lab report of carbon monoxide. If he was inhaling smoke, his bloodwork should show higher-level carbon monoxide. However, if he was dead before the fire started, he would have a lot less lung damage as he would not have been breathing to inhale deep into his lungs some of the toxins in a normal fire. His bloodwork was slightly elevated with carbon monoxide. The soot was on his face and his nose, but it hadn't entered the back of his throat or nose, suggesting that his lungs were not working at the time the soot was being created by the fire. So what killed the young man? She made a note to ask the pathologist who performed the autopsy why he thought the cause of death was smoke inhalation.

This third location was a larger fire in part because the slope of the walk was steeper. The fire would have had an easier time spreading uphill. Jill looked around at the trees, and again she could tell that the fire started in this area before picking up speed and heat. The trees next to the road were sticks, while the trees where the body was found still had some leaves on the branches. If the hiker walked to the clearing where his body was found, he had to have a certain level of fitness given the slope. Certainly, he had enough fitness to run from the fire unless he was incapacitated by something. She started thinking about what other agents might kill someone but leave little evidence. He could have been injected with succinylcholine or inhaled a gas that didn't have enough oxygen in it. Maybe he ingested a poison that was not on the routine autopsy testing list.

She was startled when she heard voices and conversation floating down to her. She called Trixie to her side and then waited to see who or what was making the noise. She waited as she spotted a couple coming downhill toward her, chatting as they walked. That was curious as she couldn't recall seeing any cars parked down below other than hers. They also gave a slight jump when they saw her, and she waited for them to approach.

"Hello," Jill said, holding tight to Trixie, who had a tendency to like strangers who seemed friendly.

"Hello. We usually don't see anyone on this trail," said the woman, advancing her hand for Trixie to sniff.

"I wondered why anyone hikes in this area. The fire wreaked such damage on the landscape here, and the smell is still bad."

"This is our favorite hike and the first time we've been here since the fire."

Jill looked around, trying to see what they saw in calling it their favorite hike.

"Why do you like this hike so much?"

"Further up the trail, there are a lot of cool rock formations, and we like testing our level of fitness in the steepness of the trail."

"Oh. Where are the rock formations?" Jill asked, looking at her watch and gauging that she could afford the time to hike farther.

"Continue about another fifteen minutes up this hill and when you're close to the top, take a right turn, and you'll find them. It was very different doing the hike today as we couldn't find our well-worn trail, and I think we climbed at a steeper rate without using the switchbacks that were here."

"Will you be back to this location to hike again?"

"We don't think so. There are other places to hike in this area, and if we wait until next spring, the landscape will look better. We might try it again at that time."

"Thanks for the hiking advice," Jill said, and the couple moved beyond her and continued their descent.

Then she thought of another question. "Hey, I didn't notice a car parked down below. How did you get here?"

The couple grinned. "A couple of years ago, we discovered a secure hiding place to stash our bikes. They are down below and chained to a small rock formation. We've been coming here for three years, and our bikes have never been stolen, I think in part because we've never seen another hiker in this area."

"Oh. Well, I wish you continued good luck in keeping your bikes hidden," Jill said with a smile.

As they disappeared, Jill said to the dog, "Well, should we go find that rock formation?" At least now she knew what the attraction was for this hiking trail.

Jill was panting by the time she reached the top and made the right turn over to the rock formation. Okay, she wasn't wowed by the gray rocks, but whatever floats your boat. Certainly, she wouldn't have ridden a bicycle uphill then hiked about a mile and a half uphill for this rock formation. There was a view, but she was unimpressed.

There really wasn't anything more to be gained from this scene. She looked at her watch and thought she had time to stop by the crime lab and talk to the pathologist who examined the victim from this scene. She was still puzzled as to what killed the man.

Jill pulled into the parking lot of the coroner's office and debated what to do with Trixie. She knew the assistant behind the desk to be dog friendly. She would see if she minded watching the dog while she went inside. If she wasn't there or wasn't available to keep Trixie behind her desk, Jill would have to wait to have questions answered about the autopsy at a later date. It was simply too hot to leave the dog in the car.

She was in luck with the assistant who was willing to take Trixie off her hands, and then she buzzed Jill through the door to the autopsy area. She didn't know the pathologist listed on the report, so she called Jennifer to see what she thought of her issue with the pathology report.

She sat down with Jennifer to discuss the inconsistencies between the evidence and the conclusion of smoke inhalation as the cause of death.

"I have to agree with you, Jill. Sadly, the report was signed off by two people in this office. Let me talk to the pathologists involved and ask them to revise their report. If they don't understand why it's wrong, I'll get them some remedial education on the subject."

"Awesome, thanks. Thinking through this last case made me think about the second one. I think it was also ruled smoke inhalation, and it should be labeled as something else. I think we have an arsonist at work here and that the arsonist is killing these victims before lighting a brushfire. Clearly, the first victim with barbiturates in his system was likely a homicide, but the second two look like accidental deaths until you look deeper into their signs and symptoms."

"Yes, I have to agree with you. Anything else I need to know?"

"I forwarded two additional cigarette butts to the crime lab for DNA analysis. All three butts may be the same cigarette brand and have been touched by the same perpetrator. I wish I could speed up the lab, but I remember how it was when I worked here. I don't suppose you've added new resources in the DNA analysis area?"

"We haven't, but we do have contracts in place to send out results for more critical case analysis. Do you think we should do it for this case? We might get results within the week."

"We are talking about three homicides. If the same DNA was on all the butts, then I would say you definitely have evidence that an arsonist is at work here. We might even luck out and identify the person if they have had their DNA registered. Arsonists start young and are usually in the criminal justice system somewhere."

"Okay, I'll route the cigarette butts to our outside contractor. Actually, your case is a good test of the company for both accuracy and turnaround time. I'll send them out and see what we get."

"Great. I'd better get back to the lobby. I stashed my dog there at reception as it was too hot to leave her in the car. I remembered your receptionist was a dog lover, and she agreed to watch while I ran the evidence down to the lab. I'm not going to do anything more on this case for a few more days as I await the DNA analysis and see if you have a new victim in several days."

"Yeah, you mentioned that pattern. I'll be watching the news."

"It's a shame we can't predict where the arsonist will strike next. Nothing is connecting the three locations other than there was something special about the hike—a rock formation, a creek, and a view. I bet there's at least a couple thousand hiking trails in this state. How could you begin to guess on which trail the arsonist will strike next? I'm not aware of any software that could do that kind of analysis for us. Besides, I bet there's something special on about fifty percent of the trails," Jill said.

"Yes, this seems pretty impossible to narrow down."

They said their goodbyes and parted ways. Soon Jill was on her way home with Trixie stretched asleep out in the back seat.

CHAPTER 6

Jill returned to work on her vineyard, giving occasional thought to the unknown arsonist. Usually, she informed her friends and teammates who lived a few states away about any cases she had, but this case felt like it was going to be all hers. Perhaps once she identified a suspect, she could pull them into the investigation.

She had a few sites she monitored for fires looking for the actions of an arsonist. With each wildfire that she read about, she had to decide if it was within an hour of a large town. It also had to be more toward the interior of California in the foothills, as that is where the three victims were found. She also worried that a body might not be immediately discovered by fire personnel given the many acres that burned and the need to walk through all those acres. There was nothing more she could do but wait for the announcement of a dead body discovered in one of many wildfires.

Today was one day beyond when the next death would have occurred, given the pattern of the last three victims. On the one hand, she was alert for a death. On the other hand, she had only a gut feeling and circumstantial evidence that an arsonist was at work. With her fear of fire, she was haunted in her dreams by fire nightmares. Nathan had shaken her awake the previous night when she'd been making little sounds of distress in her sleep.

She was planning to meet Nathan at a restaurant that they both wanted to try about an hour outside of town. He was returning from meeting a client while she was visiting a new and innovative tasting room, and they decided to try a restaurant that had good reviews in a city that they rarely visited.

She felt her phone vibrate with an incoming email or text just as she was getting into her car. Before turning on her '57 Thunderbird's ignition, she pulled the phone out to see if it was junk or something important reaching her. It was an email from Jennifer with two comments.

Spoke with our pathologist, and the death of the victim in the third case has been changed to "could not be determined."

We just got word of another victim on its way to us from a Butte County fire that fits our profile. I guess we'll see you tomorrow.

Jill replied,

Thanks for the heads up. Even though I know what you're doing, I'd love it if the mortuary techs got fluid samples and a pathologist estimate of TOD. See you early tomorrow.

Jill ended her message with a smiley face to take any sting out of her message that implied Jennifer might not know what she was doing as a forensic pathologist.

Jill started her car to head to the winery and dinner. She thought of immediately heading to Sacramento, but she knew Jennifer would have the crime scene folks start collecting any time-sensitive specimens. Canceling her dinner with Nathan wouldn't gain her additional forensic knowledge. Still, she was excited to drive north tomorrow and pursue the case.

Depending on the determination of the time of death, this might be the biggest indicator yet that the deaths were connected. She continued to think about the case as she drove to the winery she planned to tour. She had final plans for building a tasting room on her property. She'd toured wineries across the world, collecting their best features to incorporate into her new tasting room. She planned to start construction within the month, and it would be finished and ready to be used in the spring of next year. She wanted California architecture with the Italian family feel, combined with the regional pride of some wine regions. She thought her architect achieved that with the plans she'd drawn up, but the winery tasting room she was visiting had a store incorporated into it that sold whimsical wine-related products. She knew her featured wine, Moscato, was more likely to appeal to female wine drinkers than males. It made sense to have a retail store that also appealed to her future clientele.

With her mind focused on her tasting room design, she was surprised to find herself pulling into the parking lot of the winery. She had an appointment with the owner just after the tasting room closed. The parking lot was empty, so it seemed like this was still a good time for the owner.

Jill walked inside a standard Spanish arch stucco building. The owner was also a woman, and she had about five years over Jill in terms of age and experience growing grapes.

"Hi, I'm Jill Quint."

"Welcome, I'm Melissa Profino, and this is Profino Vineyards. Would you like a taste of wine while we talk?"

"You bet. What varietals do you produce?"

"Chardonnay, Cab, Zin, Pinots, and Barbera. I looked up your winery, and you like sweet, so my wines will likely not appeal to you."

"I'm trying to like dry varieties, but I'll admit I've had some awful dry wines that score high with wine enthusiasts. I planted additional crops a year ago, but they won't be ready for another couple of years, but yes, I love sugar in my wine."

"I think that's what exciting in the wine world; there's room for everyone's taste buds," Melissa said. "It's funny, but I'll try a sweet wine and think it has syrup in it. I'll pour my Cab for you."

"I'll try a dry wine and ask myself what's the difference between it and white wine vinegar. The same goes for beer. I don't like sour beer, and I wonder how the brewmaster determines that their beer has reached the perfect fermentation of a sour beer when it tastes so awful to me."

"Exactly," Melissa said, holding out her wine glass to toast.

They settled in to discuss the origin of Melissa's customers, her sales in her retail store, and staffing of the tasting room. It was a great discussion, and she was shocked when she felt her phone vibrate with a text from Nathan.

"Whoops. I forgot I was supposed to be having dinner at the Grapes Restaurant. Just a moment."

She texted Nathan with news about where she was and when she would arrive.

Melissa said, "They serve great food there, and some of my wines are on their wine list. We should stay in touch, and I'd love to tour your winery."

Jill gathered up her stuff to leave, reaching into her bag to offer Melissa a bottle of Moscato as a parting gift. "My contact information is on the bottle. Give me a call when you're in my area, and we'll make a date."

"Actually, how about tomorrow? I have to drive through your area on the way to Fresno, so I could stop by on the way there or on the return."

"Sorry, tomorrow is the one day I'm not available. I also do part-time work as a forensic pathologist and private investigator. I have to be at the Medical Examiner's Office in Sacramento tomorrow morning for some work."

"Wow! Okay, I'm going to send you an email to set up a meeting time. I'll drive out of my way just to make time. We need to talk. I'll drop you an email for a few dates next week. Oh, and here—take this bottle of Zin with you; it's the sweetest thing I have," Melissa said with a big grin.

Jill took the bottle, offered a brief handshake, and was out the door a short time later.

She drove the short distance to the restaurant and joined Nathan at his table about fifteen minutes late, leaning down to kiss him, "Sorry, I'm late."

"You're such an on-time freak that I worried when you didn't show up on time. Then I remembered that you're not deep enough into this case for me to worry about your personal safety."

"Sorry, I should have thought of that. I was having such an interesting conversation with Melissa Profino that I lost track of time. Is she one of your clients?" Jill asked.

Nathan thought through his list of clients and replied, "I don't think so. Did you like her wine label?"

"I did," and Jill reached down to pull the bottle out of her bag.

Nathan examined it and said, "I don't see a signature on this label, so I'm not sure who the wine label artist is, but I like it."

"She's going to come over to visit my winery perhaps as soon as next week. I'm not sure exactly when, but if she has time and interest, I'll bring her over to your studio."

"I wouldn't hire me if I were her. She's got a good label artist."

"She's got her act together. I liked her retail store. She's about five years ahead of me in terms of being a vintner."

"What's her background?"

"I don't know. I'll research Melissa later tonight. I do know that she likes vastly different grapes than I do, so we'll never be head-to-head competitors. She's one of the few of my fellow vintners that I liked. She's not pretentious at all. We may become good friends, although I didn't see a dog or cat nearby, and that isn't a good thing," Jill said with a smile.

"Just remember that she's operating a tasting room and may have public health standards that she can't have animals in her tasting room."

"You could be right. I hadn't thought of that. She also seemed really interested when I explained why I couldn't tour her tomorrow at my winery."

"Why can't you tour her? Did you get another fire case?" Nathan asked, frowning.

"Yes. The victim's remains are arriving tonight from Butte County. Sounds like my arsonist's M.O."

"Yikes. Are you going to have more nightmares tonight?" Nathan asked, worried. Jill wasn't afraid of much, and he'd never realized how she went out of her way to avoid fire until this case.

"I hope I don't have more nightmares. I was hoping this case might help me get over my fire paranoia."

Jill received a text and looked at her phone to see it was Jennifer. She opened the text and read it.

"The time of death of this victim was exactly spaced as though a killer was at work causing these fires. It's the best evidence yet that the deaths are not accidental. Never in California fire history have we had such similar wildfires, with single male deaths separated by exactly two weeks. These deaths cannot be victims of Mother Nature as she's a whole lot more random than that," Jill said.

"So what's the connection? Are the men related?"

"If they are related in some way, we haven't discovered that connection yet. They live in different cities, are of different ethnicities and ages. They drive different cars. I guess one thing in common is they are all hikers on a trail that promises something unique to view—a creek, a rock formation, or a panoramic view. I may have found the same brand of cigarettes at each site, and so far, two of the three men were not smokers. I don't know about the first victim as he was already buried. We're waiting on DNA analysis on those butts, which should be released any day now."

"This is sounding like you have a puppet master behind the scenes killing these men."

"Rather, it's an intelligent killer who has thought of ways of hiding their handiwork. The small mistake with the cigarettes may lead somewhere. Not only is the crime lab mystified about how these men have died, but the fire experts haven't figured out how the fires were started."

"Does anyone outside of your old office and your insurance adjustor know you're working on the case?"

"No. There's been no media coverage of the deaths, so no one is putting two and two together. It helps that this arsonist has struck in counties that aren't close to each other, so even the counties seem unaware of the trend."

"Good. With the land around your vineyard, I would like to avoid worrying about your safety from a wildfire. Let's hope your name stays out of the press. These killers have a long history of coming after you."

"I should be able to hide behind Dr. Jennifer Galloway in the coroner's office with this case."

They finished eating their very excellent dinner and made plans to meet at Jill's house later.

CHAPTER 7

$\mathcal{J}$ill was on her way to Sacramento early the next morning, having left Nathan sleeping. He wasn't a morning person, and his schedule permitted an extra two hours of sleep. She, fortunately, hadn't had any dreams the previous night of death by fire. She entered the adobe colored government-looking building just before eight. She was buzzed into the autopsy area. She changed into scrubs in the locker room before approaching the autopsy table containing the latest fire victim. Right away, she noted the similarities to the other victims in terms of age and minimal burn damage to his remains.

The pathologist who had performed the autopsy on the third victim was also assigned this one. Jill hoped that Jennifer hadn't revealed that Jill was the cause of his having to change his mode of death. It was awkward enough that Jill was a contractor looking over his shoulder. Still, she had been down this road before, and she knew how to influence the autopsy findings without getting his hackles up.

Two hours later, the autopsy was nearly finished when the pathologist said, "It appears to be another case of an undetermined mode of death. Just like the last one that was handled by this office."

"Let me ask you some questions if you don't mind." He knew that she was a pathologist who worked at one time in this very building, so whatever questions she had would likely be technical in nature.

He nodded.

"We have no signs of suicide, correct?"

"That's correct—no ligature marks, no findings of poison, no trauma."

"Could this be a death of natural causes?" Jill asked.

"No, this is too young a person to have died of natural causes."

"Was this an accident?"

The pathologist paused for a moment to think and replied, "I think that is unlikely as, again, there is no trauma. Could he have accidentally fallen asleep while a forest fire raged around him? I suppose that is possible but unlikely."

"Was this a homicide?"

"If it is, we have no idea what the murder weapon was."

"Have we done all the appropriate testing to determine what the murder weapon is?"

"You know, Dr. Quint, that's a very interesting question. I can tell you what the murder weapon isn't. It's not a knife, a gun, fire, drowning, and perhaps the top twenty poisons that we hear about in the state."

"Do you think he died of smoke inhalation?" Jill asked.

"No. While smoke particulate landed in the victim's nose and mouth, he stopped breathing before there was a lot of smoke, which is similar to the previous case. Whatever caused his death did so close to the time that the fire started."

"So if you had to make a guess at what might have killed him, that left no evidence, what would be on your list of items to include?"

"I'm starting to feel like I'm in the midst of an exam for my forensic pathology board. Do you know the answer to your question?"

"I don't. I've been thinking about what might possibly leave little evidence. The first things that come to mind are helium and nitrogen, mostly because of their ready availability. What do you think about that idea?" Jill asked.

"Well, if you breathed one-hundred percent of either gas, you would deprive yourself of oxygen. First, the victim would become unconscious, and then their heart would stop. As for lab work and how to detect either gas, I'll have to do some research, but my sense is that neither gas would show up on any chemistry or toxicology tests."

"The next question is, how would you get someone to inhale either of those gases? People like to have fun with helium, sucking in the gas from a balloon. Still, I've never seen anyone fall into unconsciousness doing that. It's possible for pure helium to quickly displace the oxygen in your lungs. Same with nitrogen-filled balloons. If he inhaled it, he would pass out even faster than with helium. Imagine if someone was trying to kill you by having you inhale from a balloon as a prank. You inhaled, and then you would become unconscious from hypoxia. Then it would be easy to place a mask over the victim's face with helium or nitrogen continuing to flow. That would kill them in a very short time. What else might have killed this victim? Can you think of any poisons?"

The pathologist was falling in line with Jill's line of thinking. He offered, "How about succinylcholine?"

"That might work. Although it can be hard to get hold of that drug, we should keep it on our list. What else can you think of?"

After running through scenarios in his head, the forensic pathologist couldn't think of another poison that wouldn't leave evidence behind in an autopsy.

"Nothing comes to mind."

"Yeah, that's been my conclusion also. So back to my original question of could this case be a homicide; the answer is may be yes, or after further investigation, the case may simply end up as 'unable to determine.'"

The two pathologists looked up as Jennifer Galloway approached holding a piece of paper in her hand.

"This is the DNA report from our outside contractor. The DNA on the three cigarette butts is the same. What is really odd is it is female. I did a quick search of the Internet to find out how many arsonists are female, and it's a small number."

"Wow, that's unusual news. Is the lab sure about the female?" Jill asked.

"Yes. In the first case, the victim's DNA was also on the cigarette butt, but the other two only had female DNA. Do we have a cigarette butt from this victim?" Jennifer asked, nodding at the victim on the autopsy table.

Jill was unaware of what evidence came in with their victim, so she waited for the pathologist to answer the question.

"I didn't see it in the evidence list. The list included the victim's clothing, a wallet, and a phone."

"I'll go visit the site tomorrow with my dog. Trixie can sniff out cigarette butts and I'll see if I can find one from the scene. That DNA report begs the question, Why is a woman killing these men?"

"That's why we hired you, Jill Quint. It's time to leave your pathology skills behind and start using your private investigator skills. However, let's speculate. We know these men are not related genetically. We know these men do not live in the same city and, in fact, live as much as two-hundred miles apart. They are all from a fairly narrow age range. My gut would say this is revenge murder by a woman, but if that were the case, there would be poison involved, and frankly, that's a cheap shot at my gender."

"I have to agree with your comments so far, Jennifer. In previous cases, I have had female murderers, but it is rare. One more thing to add to your description of these cases—the last three have died from unknown means. We know the first victim was overdosed with barbiturates, but these last three had died just before the wildfire started from an undetermined cause. So, we have a woman who has some means of taking these men out that leaves no evidence and likely doesn't require physical strength on her part as there are no signs of a struggle. You've got quite a mystery here, Dr. Galloway, and I'm looking forward to trying to solve it. I have a friend who may be able to help. She's a social media maven. She'll examine all of these men's social media posts and develop a dossier of sorts for us to review. Since she works part-time for me, I'm not sure I'll have an answer from her today, but it's likely. As for tomorrow, my dog and I will visit this latest site to see if there's any additional forensic evidence to be found. How's that sound for a plan?"

"That sounds excellent. Is there anything you need?"

"I'd like to check out a piece of clothing from the victim just in case my dog finds something else in the area besides the cigarette butt. I'd also like to see the report from the fire officials on this fire. She's starting these fires somehow. Her means of starting fires is as mysterious as her means of killing her victims."

"Okay, I'll get you both items momentarily," Jennifer said, disappearing from the autopsy suite.

Jill was left with the pathologist who looked at her and said, "This has been quite the learning experience. We have circumstantial evidence that points to homicide. I've performed autopsies on homicide victims in the past, but it's always been obvious. There have been gun or knife wounds, or lungs filled with water. Not so in this case."

"If this victim had been found sooner, we might try a lung biopsy or tracheal gas analysis or gastric gas analysis to see if the he had been near helium."

"You think the evidence is gone?"

"Yeah, though you might try gastric analysis as it would hold onto the remnants of either nitrogen or helium longer. It's worth a try, though it doesn't help us identify the killer."

"I'll do that."

Dr. Galloway returned with the items Jill requested. After changing into street clothes, she was on her way home from the Sacramento County Coroner's Office.

CHAPTER 8

$\mathcal{J}$ ill reached her house just after lunch. It was too hot to go jogging, so she made lunch and sat down at her computer to do some work on the case. She looked at the fire report to find the geocoordinates and then found the location on a map. Thanks to Google Earth, she could virtually stand on the road close to the fire and get a three-hundred-sixty degree view of the landscape. Once again, these were low foothills with gradual inclines in elevation. The closest city was Winston, and the victim lived in Oroville. She would have almost a three-hour drive to this fire location. She wondered what she would find on this hiking trail that made it interesting. Butte County was named for the nearby Sutter Buttes or small hills as they were known. The highest butte was about two-thousand feet above sea level, which was a small hill compared to the nearby Sierra-Nevada mountain range which topped ten-thousand feet. It would be another warm day, so she would have to take plenty of water for herself and the dog. Now that she knew the route she would be taking the next day, it was time to work on other things.

She composed an email to Marie, her social media maven who could find out anything about anyone. She also copied Jo, who did any financial research that she needed, and Angela, who, when on the scene of the crime, would always capture the best photographs and get the most information out of anyone they interviewed. She didn't think she would need Jo or Angela for this case, but she often was surprised by the direction a case could take. Certainly, she hadn't seen the need for Marie at the start of this investigation. A few minutes later, she had her response from Marie. She was in North Carolina, visiting her daughter and family. Since the grandkids were enthralled with a cartoon movie, she could work on Jill's investigation right away.

Jill paused for a moment to decide what to work on herself. She decided to take a deep dive into the world of female arsonists. Until she had gotten the DNA results, her nameless perpetrator had been male. It was a paradigm shift trying to understand the world of a female arsonist. There had been no DNA match in the system, so while this woman might have a history of starting fires, so far she hadn't been caught and registered into the criminal justice system.

An hour later, she understood a lot more about arsonists and some of the dreadful things they had done. The National Firefighting Organization even had the cause of some wildfires as being "wildland firefighter arson." These arsonists were motivated by their pay for fighting fires and/or the heroic feeling that came from extinguishing a fire. Those arsonists often went on long fire sprees and had a high degree of intelligence which helped them hide their crimes. Other arsonists had impulse control disorders, or they started fires to feel like they were in control.

She wondered how many of these arsonists' attributes applied to female arsonists. Clearly, the woman starting these fires was highly intelligent as she had done an amazing job hiding both the cause of death and the cause of the fire. One of the most common causes of arson fires was for insurance fraud purposes. Jill was fairly sure that insurance fraud had little to do with this series of cases she was investigating simply because the victims were not connected and the insurance claims were minimal as structures were not involved.

After reading about the arsonists, she realized she had goosebumps on her arms even though it was close to one-hundred degrees outside. Jill was the anti-arsonist as she contended with pyrophobia. She tried to imagine feeling strong and in control of fire. Instead, all she felt was that life was out of her control. A wildfire or even a house fire could overtake her at any moment. She had no control, no power over fire. It could overtake and kill her at any moment. She had no fireplace inside her house and no fire pit. She wasn't taking chances with her property when it came to fire. Maybe once they caught this arsonist, Jill should spend some time with her to help her get over her feeling of pyrophobia. They both had a psychiatric diagnosis—one had a love of fire, and the other had a fear of fire. Jill intended to put the fire out for this arsonist.

Jill spent the rest of the hour reading case studies of arsonists. Some of them had been quite prolific before they were caught. In the case she was investigating, the criminal justice system might have missed that they had a serial arsonist at work. Thankfully, the insurance adjuster, Jack, had thought to alert authorities to the potential of arson. She was lost in her thoughts about the arsonists she'd read about in the case studies. Like other serial killers, they were a creepy group of people. Fortunately, she noted the incoming email from Marie that helped extract her from the horrors of arsonists.

Sounds like you have another interesting case. I can't recall working on an arsonist in our past. Rather than doing my usual dossier on each of your victims, I instead searched for the common elements among these men. Each of them resides in a city of 50,000 people or less. They are all single because they've never married, or they're divorced. None of them have children. All of them are employed. All of them are in a similar age range. None of them indicate that they like mother nature or hiking, which is weird as it sounds like each of them died at the end of a hike. In fact, there's nothing in their profiles that says they even participate in any exercise. They live far apart, so they don't have a common restaurant or gym. They all use Facebook and Instagram. They play video games. They are all using an online dating website called Matefinder, and they play fantasy sports.

Marie continued a while longer, but Jill wondered about the dating website given that they suspected a female was their arsonist. She wrote back to Marie:

Hey, we got word that our arsonist is a female, given some evidence left at the first three sites. I'm wondering if she is finding her victims through that dating site. Can you get any additional information about it or the women the victims were chatting with?

She sat back, not expecting an immediate answer from Marie, but she smiled when she read her short response.

That's creepy.

Yes, *creepy* nicely summed up this entire case between knowing it was a female killer and then the whole fire thing. Jill spent some time studying where the victims were found as well as their home locations. It appeared that she was making her way north, skipping every other county. By Jill's estimate, the next victim would be found in Shasta County. Then she would target Del Norte County, which was small and didn't have many fires. She wondered how this woman could move around the state finding new victims. Did she live in the center of California and drive to meet these men on a hike? She would end up driving, in some cases, three or four hours. Did she torch her victims on the first or second meeting? How did she find these trails since they were in so many locations? Jill had to think she scouted them first to make sure that the location she picked had everything she needed—something special to hike for, dry brush, and no other hikers on the trail. She would also need to plan her wildfire such that it moved in the right direction over the victim yet gave her time to escape without being seen. Then she saw another text from Marie.

It's going to take me longer than I expected. I will have to create a profile and then see if I can see what women are dating the victims. I'll be Mark Simon rather than Marie Simon. I may attempt to create the profile that your arsonist likes. The good news is that even though they're dead, their profiles are still live on the website. Talk to you tomorrow.

Jill sat back and wondered what else she could do on the case but couldn't think of anything. It was time to go for a run, and she would talk with Nathan later and fix herself dinner. Then she thought of something. Had the wildfire been extinguished where they found victim number four? It had only been three days since it started, and it might not be out yet. She went to the state website on fire fighting and found that the fire was still raging. She might not be able to get close unless she could prove she had a legitimate reason to be there. She debated what to do and decided she would ask Jennifer to call her local fire leadership and see if they could clear Jill getting into the area tomorrow.

Just requesting access gave Jill heartburn. She would have to pack a mask for herself and the dog as the air was probably bad. She researched the question of how fast fires moved. This fire seemed to be moving at seven miles an hour, which might put it fifty miles away from where they found the victim depending on wind and fuel.

She was just sitting on her steps when word came back that she had access. Detective John Mullin from the California Bureau of Investigation would be joining her at the site. She was to meet the officer at a specific time and place the next day, and they would drive in together to the fire site.

She hadn't thought to tell Jennifer that the case should be investigated by the police, but she was correct in notifying them. She hadn't met this detective before. Tomorrow was going to prove to be an interesting day. With Nathan unavailable for dinner or anything else that evening, she went to bed early as she had an early drive north the next day.

CHAPTER 9

Jill was just finishing her second cup of coffee when she pulled into a convenience store parking lot to meet Detective Mullin.

She exited her car and walked over to the detective holding out her hand, "Hello, Detective Mullin, it is a pleasure to meet you. I can brief you on this case."

"We received a call from the Sacramento Coroner's Office yesterday, and it sounds like you have an interesting trend here with brushfire victims."

"I'll tell you what I know in just a moment. I drank two cups of coffee on the way here and really need to use the restroom," Jill said as she started to walk toward the store. Then she turned back and asked the detective, "Do you like dogs?"

"I do. I have two of my own at home. Would you like me to walk your dog while you go inside?"

"Let me get her for you. She's a sniffer dog, so she'll be helpful at the scene of the crime. Her name is Trixie," Jill said as she hooked the leash onto the dog and brought her over to the detective.

Jill observed for a few seconds and decided the man and the

dog were becoming fast buddies, so she went inside to take care of her own needs.

A short time later, they drove toward the fire site in an unmarked hybrid SUV vehicle. Jill discussed the forensic evidence that had been collected so far. She also mentioned the work that Marie was doing regarding the dating app. Trixie was asleep in the back of the vehicle, but she sprang up once she felt the vehicle slow at a law enforcement checkpoint near the fire. Detective Mullin held out his business card. After a short discussion, they continued down the road less than a mile to the site of the fourth victim's demise.

Jill got out of the vehicle with her backpack containing everything she needed to investigate the fire scene and the usual water for the dog.

"Each location in which a victim has been found has had something special going for it as a hiking trail. The first case had a spectacular view. The second case was a beautiful creek, and the last case had an interesting rock formation. As we approach the scene, ask yourself, what makes this hike special?"

The detective nodded and said, "At this point, you think all four deaths are homicide, the killer is a female arsonist, who is finding her victims on a dating app, and one of their dates includes a special hike where she has some technique to incapacitate her gentleman before she starts a wildfire, right?"

"When you put it that way, it sounds very far-fetched, but that's my theory at the moment. This female arsonist is good at covering her tracks. Still, she's making a few mistakes, and let's hope that leads us to her before she kills her next victim in eleven days in Shasta County."

"I think I missed your explanation as to why she'll strike in eleven days and in Shasta County. That sounds exact. Explain, please."

"It's the pattern of these deaths. She strikes every two weeks in a county that is two counties north of where she killed her last victim."

"Dr. Quint, you're scaring me. This potential killer sounds smart and determined."

"Detective, do you really think these cases are not related and are not homicide? You also know from your law enforcement training that successful serial killers are highly intelligent. They have to be to escape notice and capture by law enforcement. I've never had a case involving an arsonist, so I've done quite a bit of reading about them to understand why they start fires. This arsonist feels very satisfied every time she starts a fire. It's a moment of control and power. She's pleased she had the control to start the fire and the power to control the spread, so not only does it kill her victim, but it leaves her unscathed."

"I'll have to read up on arson when I return to my computer. According to my phone, we're coming upon the murder scene."

Jill tried to imagine what the area looked like before the fire turned everything black and gray. Like the other fire locations, it looked bleak, and it stunk. The air was unhealthy, and the two humans and the dog had masks on trying to filter the air. Jill would have to remove Trixie's mask when she was ready for the dog to go to work, but in the meanwhile, she wanted to keep the dog safe from the bad air.

Jill studied the geocoordinates and eyed in her mind their approximate circle. She pulled the pack of cigarettes out of her backpack and put latex gloves on.

"Trixie, smell," Jill said to the dog, holding out a cigarette in her gloved hand from the pack that she purchased before visiting the first fire victim site.

"Trixie, find." Jill commanded the dog to search for the cigarette butt that she thought might connect this case to the others. The dog moved back and forth across the area for a long time. It seemed like she wasn't going to find a butt, but after some fifteen minutes, she finally focused on a spot, and Jill approached to see if the dog had found anything. Using her tool and with Detective Mullin leaning over the area, Jill began gently moving the fire debris to see if the dog had found anything.

"There," said Detective Mullin, pointing to what looked like a butt.

Jill brought out her tweezers and grabbed the item in question, putting it into a specimen bag.

"What do you want to do with this? The Sacramento Coroner's Office sent the last three butts out to a private DNA lab and got results in about three days. Either you or I could drop off this specimen there. If you have an alternate lab to process it, then we'll have to get the other butts and have your lab process all four of them."

"I prefer to send it to the same lab as the other three butts. I know this case is not the Sacramento coroner's case as it is a Butte County victim. If there's a problem with the cost of the test, my agency will cover it. I'll drop this specimen off with Dr. Galloway."

Jill nodded and then pulled out a piece of clothing from their fourth victim and repeated the same routine she went through with Trixie to find the cigarette butt. She wanted the dog to sense the victim's scent in case he had touched anything else in this fire zone. Close by to where they were kneeling, the dog found additional evidence. It was a piece of latex balloon.

"I'm surprised this didn't melt in the fire."

"It might have. Does it have the same elasticity as your average balloon?" asked the detective.

Jill dug around a little more and then said, "Maybe something in the wildfire area protected it. Since this is where the fire started, it might not have been as hot as the fire is now since it's been under way for several days. This is a really important piece of evidence as we believe that our killer is disabling these men with perhaps helium or nitrogen gas."

"How does that work? How do helium and nitrogen kill people? Is it quick?"

"You may die in less than a minute breathing these gases. Pure helium or nitrogen will displace the oxygen in your lungs. You will die of hypoxemia, or low oxygen in the blood. You will be unconscious after about thirty seconds. Then your major organs will shut down as they detect the lack of oxygen. It's a fairly popular way to commit suicide as it's painless and usually not reversible. You can buy helium at a party supply store, but it's diluted with air. You can buy pure helium and nitrogen from industrial suppliers as it is used in welding."

"What do you want to test this balloon for?" asked the detective.

"There may be DNA on it, and we should be able to detect from the residual what kind of gas was in the balloon before it burst."

"What would that tell us?"

"It would give us a cause and mode of death if we knew these guys were inhaling helium. With that, you would have the murder weapon. It won't help in identifying our arsonist, but you would have confirmation of homicide, not a suicide or accidental death, with these cases."

"Why couldn't this be an accidental death?" asked the detective, though the way he asked it suggested he knew the answer to his own question.

"Where's the source of the helium? If you knock yourself unconscious with helium or nitrogen gas, where did it come from? Someone else had to be here watching you inhale the gas so they could take the canister away once you were dead. Is that the scenario you saw in your imagination?" Jill asked.

"Are all four deaths from inhaling a gas?"

"No. She killed the first man by putting barbiturates in a mojito drink."

"We've got a smart woman on her hands. She's doing an excellent job of hiding her identity and hiding the fact that these are murders and not accidents."

"I think we're done collecting evidence here. Trixie hasn't alerted us that there's any additional evidence. Now we need to find out what the attraction is with this trail. So I'm going to put her mask back on. And we'll walk up that hill and see what's at the top. Can you check for anything else that might be interesting in this area? Identifying whatever is special about this trail is the last piece of forensic evidence that we will find at the scene."

The detective nodded, and they parted ways to explore the area around where their victim was murdered. Jill found a small pond and decided that the feature was likely what made this hiking trail special. That is, unless the detective found something more interesting.

After exploring the area, they joined together to walk back to the car. The detective hadn't found anything unusual in his walk around the murder scene, so they agreed that the pond must be the attraction. When Jill got home, she planned to research this hiking trail to see what people said about the trail and how crowded it might be. She bet that someone somewhere wrote that they never saw another human on the hiking trail, and that would be the attraction to their arsonist. They passed through the law enforcement checkpoint and returned to where Jill's car was parked at the convenience store. They tossed ideas back and forth about how they would identify and capture this arsonist. Still, the reality was they had so little information about her identity that, at this point, it was like looking for a needle in a haystack.

Before the detective drove away, Jill noticed she had an email from Marie that had been holding out in cyberspace, waiting for Jill's phone to reconnect to the Internet. She read the message from Marie and then told Detective Mullin, "My friend, the social media maven, did not find a single woman in common with the profiles for all four victims."

The detective nodded, seemingly not surprised that Jill's friend

Marie came up with nothing. He had low expectations of them from the start, just like she remembered in a previous case with domestic terrorists. She and her friends hadn't been to any law enforcement academy. What did they know about finding criminals?

"I think you should get a search warrant for that dating app company looking for any women that were deleted from the profiles of the victims on the day they were murdered."

"Do you?" asked the detective with a sarcastic tone.

He had seemed cooperative and professionally respectful earlier in their examination of the crime scene. Maybe he had just been buying his time until he squeezed all the information out of her and the dog. Jill sighed and thought about describing her marvelous feats in crime-solving despite her lack of being a detective, but she knew her breath would be wasted. Past experience has rarely resulted in a change in attitude. She just walked away from the detective and got in her car to head home.

"Well, Trixie girl, he may have liked dogs, but he was still a knucklehead," Jill said to the dog as she pulled out of the convenience store parking lot for the long drive home. Jill looked in the rear-view mirror and noted the dog's response was to fall asleep to her comment.

CHAPTER 10

Jill was driving home, thinking about the case and what more she could do to help the investigation along. The more she thought about it, the more she felt that these murders were typical of a female killer. All of the men had had a gentle death. That is, if you could call death fifty years before your time *gentle*. If the test results came back that the men inhaled helium or nitrogen, then they went to their death through unconsciousness rather than feeling the pain of a stab or a bullet tearing through their body.

She was focused on the dating site as the source for where the woman found multiple victims in different geographical locations. These men offered such disparate profiles. They didn't meet at work or school or church, or a community group. Instead, they met in the online community.

She wondered how many women were on the site, and she planned to create an account when she got home to examine the people on this dating website. She also wanted to search the region of Shasta County and see how big the pool of men was. She had about twelve days before the next death to prevent the next man from becoming the arsonist's latest victim. She wanted to also come up with a name for the woman as she was tired of calling her the arsonist. Maybe she would call her the Burnt Widow. She'd ask Nathan's marketing brain to give her a catchy name.

She gave Trixie a bath outside once they reached home as they both had remnants of the fire zone on them. Jill felt smoky even though she'd kept her mask on the entire time they were in the fire zone. The smoke was in her hair and on her clothing. Once she was done washing the dog, she took a look around to make sure no one was nearby, then she did a quick strip and left her clothes on the porch, running upstairs to hop into the shower. She thought about going for a run, but after six hours in the car and the need to take a shower after arriving home, she passed on the run. Maybe she would check with Nathan and see if he would be up to a little martial arts practice. She practiced Tai Chi, and he was a master black belt in Hapkido. His house contained a nice dojo that would be perfect for practice. She'd like to kick a bag to work out her frustration with yet another law enforcement officer who believed she didn't belong in an investigation.

She spent some time on the dating app reading the profiles of the men. She didn't know the four victims, but she wouldn't want to get to know them by their profiles. They had typos in their profiles, weren't interested in physical activity, and said their ideal date was meeting in a bar. The kindest thing she could say about the victims was they were non-smokers. She wondered how the Burnt Widow had talked these men into hiking. She questioned if hiking was their first date or a subsequent date. What motivation did she provide to get the men to hike? Perhaps it was the oldest motivation in the book—outdoor sex. She planned to show the profiles to Nathan and get a man's opinion on motivation and male attitude.

A short time later, Jill and Trixie entered Nathan's house to find him cooking in the kitchen. Arthur, Nathan's cat, gave Trixie his usual *I hate dogs* stare, which had the Dalmatian looking away in intimidation. Jill smiled as she came around the kitchen counter to kiss Nathan.

"Some things never change. You're a wonderful cook and a great kisser, and my dog is afraid of your cat after a single glare."

Nathan chuckled, "Arthur has mastered that glare, and yet he only uses it on Trixie."

"Oh well, she worked hard today sniffing out evidence in a very smoky site. Since she was strong there, I won't worry about her being strong elsewhere in her life. I need you to look at a dating site, and I wondered if we could use your dojo after dinner. I feel the urge to kick."

"Okay, that was a paragraph of random thoughts that I didn't follow. I understand you want to kick in my dojo. Yes, we can do that. Did you say you need me to look at a dating site? Why would I ever do that?"

"I do tend to blurt out stuff, don't I? My four victims used the dating site, Matefinder, and I want you to look at the victims' profiles. I found the men undatable, but that's an opinion of one."

"Okay. I'll be curious to see what your taste in men is not, according to the profiles of these four men. Seems like I better not make those mistakes," Nathan said with a chuckle.

"Error number one: don't have typos in your profile. I'm talking about typos that look like you clearly don't know how to spell, not fingers slipping on the keyboard."

"In my business life, I can't afford to have typos. Nothing gets you fired faster."

"I never thought about that before, but how do you make sure all of your materials are typo-free?"

"It's a combo of my assistant, Artificial Intelligence programs, and myself. Both my assistant and I attended a course that teaches you copyediting, and it gave us a few tools to use."

"That makes sense. Second, don't make our first date at a noisy bar. Not a bar and restaurant establishment, but a grungy bar."

"Got that, and I would likewise be put off seeing both of these profile problems in a female as well."

"Have you ever used an online dating platform?" Jill asked, curious about his dating life.

"Perhaps a decade ago, but there are so many women within a certain range that you're looking for—no typos, common interests, and age—that it's depressing to narrow them down. My first date was always in a coffee house of some sort. That way, there was enough activity to keep some kind of flow going, and the women and I would feel safe. I also like to observe someone's manners as those are important too."

"What made you give it up?"

"Too many bad first dates."

"Ditto. It's obviously a system that works, but I lack the patience for it."

"I can imagine," Nathan said, grinning at Jill. He knew from her urgency to solve cases that she could have an extreme streak of impatience, but then he thought of something.

"Wait, you've been very patient, taking years to get your tasting room built and operational. You have patience when you need to."

"I'm much more patient when it comes to the business of growing grapes. You have to be. You spend years growing vines to get your first vintage, then months every year growing subsequent vintages. If you're not careful, you could lose it all to some pest. I would also say I can be extremely patient when it comes to mixing grapes to get the perfect barrel of wine."

"True. What's third on your list of undesirable qualities?"

"Someone who doesn't enjoy physical activity and the outdoors. I can't imagine spending time around someone who doesn't want to explore nature's bounty."

"I agree with you as well. Seems like we would have been a match. What specifically do you want to look at with these guys' profiles? If you've already established that they're not datable material," Nathan asked.

"I want to make sure that I hadn't missed anything good about these guys."

"How does that relate to your case? I can't always follow that detective mind of yours."

"So, here's my premise: We have a female arsonist who uses this dating site to murder random men who have Matefinder profiles that are awful, in my opinion. None of the men indicated they had an interest in hiking. So how did she get them to agree to meet her? They did agree to meet her for a hike as their vehicles are always found afterward. Was the hike the first or second or third date?"

"Ah. I would guess it's at least the second or third date. No dude with no interest in hiking is going to make that the first date. What woman would be willing to go off on a deserted hiking trail with a man she's never met? Nothing says I don't care for my personal safety than that, and from what you've said about this arsonist, she cares for her personal safety. Otherwise, she probably would have lit herself on fire by now."

"See, that's what I like about the way you think," Jill said with a smile. "Should I set the table for dinner? Afterwards, we can look at my profiles. By then, our food will have settled, and I can kick a certain detective's face to my heart's desire later in your dojo."

"Yes, set the table; dinner is almost ready. Maybe we can find some other, more cheerful topic to discuss. Read any good books recently?"

Jill laughed and said, "How about if we talk sports. Isn't that a relaxing topic?

"You're too singularly focused on football. I dare you to hold a conversation on baseball."

"You've got me there. I know nothing about the SF Giants or the Oakland A's. How about we compromise with basketball? I can somewhat hold a conversation there."

Nathan laughed as he began to plate their dinner while Jill poured the wine he'd had breathing.

In the end, they talked about the two classes Nathan was teaching at the University. He had his first class in the past day and had loved it.

"The students were more engaged than I expected. It seems everyone wants to graduate and become my competitor. They see it as a skill they can offer a winery looking for a manager. I asked them what they planned to do with the lessons from this class, and those were the two main answers."

"That's a strong motivation if they can see the point in taking a class. I remember a basic biology class that I hated in college. There is something called the Krebs cycle, which is the key metabolic pathway that connects carbohydrate, fat, and protein metabolism. There's a bunch of oxygen, hydrogen, and carbon molecules and some enzymes that change over nine steps. We had to memorize those nine steps for a test, getting all the molecules correct. I hated that. The Krebs cycle was discovered in the 1930s and had been in textbooks forever. Why couldn't we just understand what it was and look it up in a textbook when we needed the actual cycle steps? I never saw any motivation to memorize that. In fact, I did poorly on the exam as I was stubbornly mad that the professor wanted it memorized."

"You actually did poorly on an exam?" Nathan asked, knowing that medical school was academically rigorous.

"Yep. After the poor grade and the realization that I was potentially hurting my entire future career, I put up and shut up. So as a past student, I would have so appreciated the practical knowledge you're teaching rather than requiring your students to memorize the wine varietal table to do marketing."

"Who says I'm not going to do that?"

"You're far too kind a man to be that mean."

"Is that another thing you look for in a dating profile?"

"Yes, speaking of which, let's go review the profiles," Jill said.

Jill logged into her account so she could show Nathan the four victim profiles. She leaned back quietly, sipping her wine, while Nathan reviewed each of the profiles.

"Sometimes, I'm astounded by the lack of substance in my fellow man or woman. Do none of these men understand that the summation of their profiles would lead one to think they have nothing to offer a woman? They are all vampires willing to suck the life out of any woman they date."

"It's a good way to put it. I like your term *vampires*. What motivation can you think of that would have gotten these four men to go for a hike? Nothing in their profile says they like hiking, or physical exercise, or the great outdoors."

"I can think of only one thing. Do you have a detailed list of what was found with the men? A list of their personal possessions?"

"I do. What am I looking for?"

"Let me see."

Jill spent a moment bringing up the autopsy reports of the four victims. Included with each victim was a list of whatever they came in with—clothing, phone, car keys. It was whatever they had in their pockets and on their person at the time of their death.

Nathan looked through the four lists and just shook his head.

"What?" Jill asked with an aggrieved voice. What was he shaking his head over?

"I can think of only one thing that could get these men to voluntarily walk on a hike in a remote area, and that is the promise of sex. I was looking for a condom in the list of possessions but didn't see that any of your victims have protection with them. Maybe my judgment was wrong, and that's not what they were up to, but it's the only motivation I can think of with these four men in particular. Maybe I shouldn't be surprised as they come across as irresponsible men, and planning to go into the woods for sex with a strange woman further proves their profile. Is that what you wanted to hear?"

"That was actually my theory also as I couldn't think of any other motivation to get them into the woods. I suppose she could have bribed them with money and then taken it back once they were unconscious. I know we didn't find cash with any of the victims. That could be a sign of the times with everyone purchasing with debit cards, or it could be because she cleaned them out before she set the fire. After all, why needlessly burn up cash?"

They talked a little bit more about motivation and her victims but couldn't think of another reason other than the one they had. They spent some time working on their individual martial arts in Nathan's dojo before heading to bed. Jill felt better for having kicked and punched the detective's imaginary face. Still, she had no solution to improving her relationship with the detective. Again, Nathan had to wake Jill up in the middle of the night as she was clearly having a nightmare trying to escape a fire in her dreams.

CHAPTER 11

*J*ill debated driving into Sacramento, but she couldn't think of anything she could do there that she couldn't do at home. She was determined to get a run in early before the heat climbed too much. She put her running clothes on and stepped outside with Trixie to stretch, and she sniffed the air. Was it her imagination, or was there a fire close by? She called the general number for her local law enforcement and asked if there was an active wildfire in the county.

"Yes, ma'am. We had a brushfire break out in the middle of the night after some dry lightning strikes. It's burned about one-thousand acres, and it's not under control. What's your address?"

Jill gave the dispatcher her home address.

"Ma'am, you're about ten miles as the crow flies from the active fire. The good news is the aqueduct is between your land and the fire, and the aqueduct will serve as a barrier to the fire spreading your way. I need to go now unless you have further questions."

Jill ended the call after giving her thanks for the information. She wasn't as sure as the dispatcher that the aqueduct would serve as a good barrier. The California aqueduct was 444 miles of concrete river that moved water from Northern California through the rich agricultural growing area of central California and continued south to Southern California. In her area, the aqueduct was forty feet wide. Brushfire sparks with a little wind could easily transverse from one side of the aqueduct to the other.

Trixie was getting impatient to run, but Jill wanted to look at a map to refresh her memory of where the fire was burning. She certainly didn't want to run in that direction as the air would get progressively worse. She studied where things were burning and thought it unlikely that her vineyard was at risk. According to the weather forecast, the wind was blowing away from her land. In addition to the aqueduct, a wide four-lane highway offered some barrier to the fire. Also, where it likely was burning at the moment was a low foothill heading into Yosemite National Park. That would also keep the fire burning away from Jill's land. Her biggest worry would be smoke damage to her grape crop. Some vineyards had found their grapes to be smoke damaged and unusable after nearby fires. Certainly, wine drinkers did not want a smoky flavor to their Moscato wine.

The worry about the smoke and fire made Jill cut her run short as she worried about the fire's direction and the smoky air. Instead of running four to five miles, she was done after two miles. She returned home and showered, then she checked on the fire through various sources. Her vineyard was still safe and would likely stay safe as the land scorched at the beginning of the fire was now a barrier to the fire coming back her way. Still, she was tempted to get in her car and drive to the location of the fire just to make sure it couldn't switch directions and come her way. She texted Nathan her knowledge about the fire. She knew she could evacuate to his property, and he replied to her message with that same invitation.

He asked the question she had been vaguely thinking about:

Was this wildfire the work of your arsonist?

She hoped not because that meant they would soon find a

dead body among the debris of the scorched earth from the fire. She spent a good hour writing out a fire evacuation plan. She made one a couple of years ago, but now she had more equipment and land to worry about. If she had to leave her land, what would she do? Beyond keeping herself and the dog safe, what else did she need? So, she made a checklist with the basics like records, computer technology, and clothes. The more she thought about her fire evacuation plan, the more she made a note to herself to buy a trailer. Her barn that she used for forensic testing was filled with expensive equipment. If she had a trailer, she could load it with her analyzers and probably most of her barrels of wine. It wouldn't be good for the wine to move it from her cool wine cellar to the hot Central Valley air knowing that the barrels would be shaken at the very time they were supposed to be left alone to age to perfection. The heat and motion might destroy the entire vintage, but then the fire could also do that. She had a forklift that could lift the analyzers for her into a trailer bed. Yes, she would watch the fire, and when it was out, she would go shopping for that trailer.

She went outside to her barn and sat there looking at the analyzers. Might she take this opportunity to do something different with her consulting business? Should she think about getting a trailer to hold her wine barrels? Maybe. She wondered if she could get one of those large vans that she sometimes saw plumbers or electricians use to cart around their supplies. What if she found one big enough that it could carry the analyzers she needed to run specimens for her cases? About half of her work was inside the state of California, and she could drive the van to the crime scene. Really, she could probably cover the West Coast with the van. This brilliant idea, as far as she was concerned, deserved more research. She would want a used van as she would end up taking it to a crime scene a little less than once a month. She didn't need a new vehicle to do that.

She wrote herself a note to follow up on the idea and headed into her kitchen to get a drink, coughing a little as she went. The air was bad outside, though not as bad as the previous day when she visited the crime scene for victim number four.

After she ended the coughing fit, she returned to her computer to see if there was an email from Jennifer Galloway. The lab should have had time to analyze the balloon fragments and determine what gas had been inside the balloon. The cigarette butt would take another day or two to see if it matched the other three butts.

She checked in with Jennifer to see if she had a report yet. Once Jennifer gave her the analysis of the balloon fragment, she planned to tell her about the Matefinder website as a possible source of victims. Jill was operating somewhat in a gray zone as she had been hired to help oversee the three fire victim cases. Instead, she was stepping into the area of Detective Mullin.

Jill got a quick response from Jennifer and, after reading it, looked at her computer screen with dismay. Detective Mullin had not delivered the evidence to Dr. Galloway's lab. She wondered what he had done with the forensic evidence. There was nothing she could do other than call and ask. Maybe he had a faster source for analysis, though she doubted it. It was a simple analysis of the balloon; it was one that she could've done with the equipment in her barn. It would've taken Jennifer's staff less than thirty minutes to come up with an answer.

She pulled out his card and dialed the number. Her call went to voicemail, so she left a message. She hadn't heard that his division had its own crime lab to process forensic evidence. Maybe he was cooperating with the FBI or some other agency. She took a moment to explore the directory, and she didn't find his name anywhere. She dropped the card into an envelope so she wouldn't leave any fingerprints on it. Her sixth sense was buzzing. She called the State Bureau of Investigation and began talking to people. Thirty minutes later, she was deeply puzzled. Who was Detective John Mullin? Was he even working in law enforcement?

Was he a private detective like herself? Surely he'd shown some form of ID to the Sacramento Coroner's Office in order to get inside.

She called Jennifer Galloway to ask her about the conversation with the detective.

"Have you met him in prior cases?"

"No. Why?"

"I was puzzled as to why he didn't bring the forensic evidence to you from our tour of the crime scene for victim number four yesterday. Your lab is the biggest and most sophisticated lab around. I used his card and called him, but I just got a voicemail. So, I started asking the staff at the CBI, and there is no Detective Mullin in their office."

"That's really strange. How would he know enough about the case to stop by our office?"

"Would anyone have checked his identification other than the business card? Anyone can create a business card. Did he have a shield? Though come to think of it, I think he held out a business card at the fire checkpoint."

"Okay, this case is suddenly getting strange, Jill. We didn't hire you to make it strange."

"Hey, it's not my fault. The detective is the one who didn't give you the evidence we collected yesterday."

"I'm going to call you back after I talk to the staff here. I want to know if someone did check his badge. I should be able to call you back in about ten minutes. Will you be there?"

"Sitting by the phone, waiting for your call."

The phone call ended, and Jill leaned back in her chair, trying to think of her prior cases. Had she ever encountered someone impersonating a peace officer in order to get more information about the case? What was his relationship to the female arsonist, or was there one? All she could do was wait for Jennifer to call her back.

Jill stood up and paced, waving her arms like a windmill. The strange news about the detective had caused her shoulders to seize up. She was doing what she could to relax, but this was an unusual circumstance.

As soon as her phone rang, she hit the connect button.

"This is Jill."

"Our receptionist allowed him inside two days ago based on his business card. She did not ask to see his shield, and we've corrected that. I've asked our security personnel to pull footage from that day. We hope to come up with his identity and find out what he is doing in the middle of a murder case stealing and tampering with forensic evidence."

"Did you call his office to request law enforcement?"

"No. He showed up, and I was like, 'Duh, I should have thought of that.'"

"That's what I thought when you mentioned his involvement. I'm going to look through my phone. I took a lot of pictures yesterday, and I'm fairly sure I got one of him."

Jill put her phone on speaker and started searching through her phone. She found several pictures, but the "detective" had turned his face away in each photo.

"Jennifer, I have a couple pictures with him in it, but he turned his head either down or away from the camera, so they are no good. Can you check your camera outside the front door to see if you have anything?"

"I will, but I doubt I have anything as I remember him wearing a ball cap with the embroidered letters *CBI*."

"I can't remember working with the CBI when I worked there as a medical examiner. Have you worked with them on a case before?"

"No. I'll admit I actually never heard of the CBI, and so I looked up the agency after the detective was here, but I didn't specifically look for him."

"Can you take a look at him on tape and also ask your staff if he touched anything while in your building? Probably any surface he touched one-hundred other people have touched since then, which will prevent you from collecting fingerprint impressions."

"Are all of your cases this weird, Jill? In my twenty years as a medical examiner, I've yet to meet a fake law enforcement officer. Of course, I've never identified a female arsonist either. Still, I do love a good mystery. Let me know how I can help as I'm not sure where to go with this information."

"For a start, you should call your local law enforcement—either the Sacramento County Sheriff or the Sacramento Police Department—as at the very least you have law enforcement officer impersonation. Besides, we should have a real detective involved with these cases. You could leave it up to the city or county police to determine who has jurisdiction since none of these deaths occurred within their county."

"Good idea. Are you available to come to Sacramento today? You should be involved with the conversation as we try to enumerate the multiple issues with this case."

Jill thought about her plans for the day and couldn't think of anything that couldn't be rescheduled.

"I can be there. Text me when you have time. It will take me ninety minutes to get there."

"I think I'll insist on a meeting with law enforcement in exactly two hours. That should be plenty of time for them to assign officers to this case. See you soon."

Jill affirmed she would be there, and they ended their call. She agreed with Jennifer that this case kept getting weirder. Why would this man have knowledge of their case? It had not been announced to the media that an arsonist was on the loose, killing men and starting wildfires. Now he knew as much information as anyone about the case. No wonder he had such a sarcastic reply to her request to get a search warrant. As a fake lawman, he had no access to search warrants.

CHAPTER 12

Jill pulled into the parking lot at the medical examiner's building, and there were a few more cars in the parking lot. She figured that Jennifer had rallied the troops for the upcoming meeting. She was buzzed into the building and then buzzed through the second door that would allow her to reach the conference room. When she entered, Jennifer was already there with files in front of her. There were also a male and another female, and she figured those were the detectives.

Jennifer said, "This is our former forensic pathologist and now consultant, Dr. Jill Quint. Jill, this is Detective Kelly Maguire from SPD and Detective Aaron Rodriguez from the Sheriff's Department. We're expecting a representative of the FBI momentarily."

Jill reached across the table to shake their hands and pass out her business card. She didn't know either of the detectives. They were both on the young side and perhaps had made detective after she worked for this office.

Someone else entered the room directed there by one of Jennifer's staff. He said, "Hi, I'm Special Agent Brandon Sanderson from the Sacramento office of the FBI."

Further introductions were made, and they got down to business.

Jennifer started, "About two or three weeks ago, I received a call from a fire insurance investigator pointing out the similarity of three lone males who have died in brushfires in different counties. We had the third victim in our morgue. When I received that phone call, we were dealing with the mass casualty of the bus crash out on the highway. Dr. Quint and I used to work together, and I know she provides opinions on the cause of death and is a licensed private investigator. I asked her to review the three cases to see if any of them needed to be reclassified as a homicide. Up to that point, they were considered accidental deaths. She visited the three wildfire sites, reviewed the remains of the victim in our morgue, and reviewed the reports of the first two victims, which were not handled by this office. None of the deaths have occurred in Sacramento County; however, we back up smaller counties when they lack the resources. Dr. Quint collected forensic evidence of cigarette butts close to the victims in the first two scenes. With the third scene, the victim arrived here with that piece of forensic evidence.

"We sent the butts out for DNA analysis. All the fire victims were male, but the DNA taken from the cigarette was female, and it was the same at all three sites. We do not have a cause of death for the second two victims. The first victim was determined to have alcohol and barbiturates in his stomach contents. So his death was ruled a suicide initially. The second two victims did not have alcohol or barbiturates, nor did they die by smoke inhalation. They were dead before the fire started. The fire marshal was unable to determine what started the fire. So other than coincidence, we don't have much linking these cases. Dr. Quint predicted that if we had a serial arsonist at work, the fourth victim would die about three days ago. This office got a call from Butte County asking for assistance with a male found within a wildfire zone."

Jennifer took a sip of water as the explanation was drying out her throat.

"Dr. Quint visited the site of the fourth victim yesterday. And here's where the case gets weird. The day before, this office was visited by Detective John Mullin from the California Bureau of Investigation. The forensic evidence collected at the scene was supposed to be brought to this office yesterday by the detective as the CBI doesn't have a crime lab. When Dr. Quint inquired this morning as to the test results of that forensic evidence, that was when we noted that the detective hadn't stopped by here yesterday. This morning Dr. Quint called him to find out where the evidence was and got his voicemail. She then worked her way through the CBI and learned that there isn't a detective named John Mullin working there. He has all the details of this case as Dr. Quint discussed it with him, but at this time, he appears to be impersonating law enforcement."

The three law enforcement people had been taking notes while Jennifer talked about the case, and she'd given so much information that they were still writing even though her explanation had ended. Jennifer placed a copy of John Mullin's business card in a clear plastic bag on the conference table. They all took a look at the card.

"First question, what agency should handle this case?" Jennifer asked.

"I think the law enforcement impersonation took place within the city and county of Sacramento, so that would be under our jurisdiction. It appears we also have evidence tampering. Do you have any theories as to why the man showed up when he did? I don't recall hearing about these three deaths due to arson or even some other cause on the news. How did he know about that, and how did he know this office was performing the autopsy on one of the victims? As none of the fires occurred in this county, you wouldn't automatically think to head to the Sacramento Medical Examiner's Office," said Detective Aaron Rodriguez.

"Can we back up and talk about these three cases?" asked Agent Sanderson. "Tell me more about why all four cases are connected. These deaths occurred perhaps one-hundred miles apart and two weeks apart?"

Jill spoke for the first time, "Yes, that's correct. Let me tell you about the four victims as they have one thing in common. They are all on a dating site called Matefinder. None of the men are smokers. This is based on both their social media profiles and testing for nicotine in their blood, and yet cigarette butts were found next to their remains. The first three fires have occurred on documented hiking trails. The trails are reviewed by hikers who say they are deserted, and there was something special on the hike. In the case of the first wildfire, there was a beautiful view before everything was torched. There was a beautiful creek with the second wildfire, and the third wildfire had an interesting rock formation. I think a pond might be the point of interest for the fourth hiking trail. All of the men were either Caucasian or Hispanic and between thirty-five and forty-five years of age. Each of their social media profiles suggested they were couch potatoes, unlikely to take random hikes in the woods.

"At this time, we don't know what killed them. We just know the victims expired before the fire started."

"How do you know that?" asked one of the detectives.

"While they had the remnants of smoke inside their nose and mouth, there is no evidence in their lungs of inhaling smoke. That means they were dead before the fire started. A piece of evidence that we found yesterday was a part of a balloon. Our female arsonist could have had victims inhale nitrogen or helium, killing them and leaving very little evidence. At this point, we no longer have the balloon fragment, and so the theory of an inert gas killing them is just speculation at this point."

"I think you have enough evidence for us to open an investigation," said Agent Sanderson. "I'd like to work with my colleagues here, Detectives Rodriguez and Maguire."

"Based on what you've said, the arsonist is going to strike again in eleven days. Is that correct?" asked Detective Maguire.

"That seems to be the schedule she's on. She should kill her next victim in Shasta County in four days in a wildfire."

"Wow," remarked Rodriguez.

"Why do you say Shasta County, Dr. Quint?" asked Agent Sanderson.

"If you see the pattern of the crime scenes, you will note that each county is two over from the previous county. So, she killed in Butte, she'll skip Tehama or Plumas and kill someone in Shasta or Lassen County. My money's on Shasta County as she likes foothills to kill in, and she needs a population to select her victim from. The city of Redding is just under 100,000 residents. Still, Lassen County is small. Its largest city, Susanville, has about 17,000 residents, and two-thirds of them work at one of the three prisons. Maybe your FBI profile people could figure out where she's going to strike next?"

"We might be going down the wrong path. Maybe these cases aren't connected. Maybe they're all victims of random bad luck if you can't determine what killed them," said Detective Maguire. "Don't we have a fair number of homeless living and campfire cooking in our wildfire areas? They start fires every year."

"That's entirely possible. However, you have a fake cop who has inserted himself into this case, and that should bother you as he's walked away with some prime evidence," Jill said, mad that for what felt like the one-hundredth time, she was not being taken seriously because she wasn't a cop.

"You're right, Dr. Quint, and I was briefed by the Special Agent in Charge of Northern California that no matter how wild your story is to believe you and help you," said Agent Sanderson. "I think your story qualifies as wild, and I believe you."

"Thank you," Jill said, turning her body away from Detective Maguire because she was done with the detective.

"Do you have any security tapes of the fake detective John

Mullin entering or walking around the facility?" asked Detective Rodriguez.

"We have him on security tape, but he keeps his head down, and he's wearing a ballcap, so it's not much help."

"I have facial recognition software that can identify someone, but I need a full face, and we don't seem to have that here. I also took pictures of John Mullin yesterday at the wildfire site, and in all of my pictures, he has his head turned away from the camera lens. I don't believe we have a solid photograph we can use to identify him," Jill said.

Jennifer nodded, "Agent Sanderson, I'll turn the tapes over to you."

"I'd like a copy as well," said Rodriguez. He apparently believed Jill's explanation from what she could tell, or at least he wanted to find the fake cop.

Jill was thinking about how she could move on without the evidence that John Mullin walked away with the previous day.

"I have a trained scent dog, and she discovered the cigarette butts and the balloon fragment at the fire location for the fourth victim. At the wildfire locations for victims two and three, I didn't have her search for anything from the victims. Jennifer, if you can get me a personal effect of victims two and three, I'll take Trixie out to the fire scenes again and have her search. Maybe we'll luck out."

"I'd like to go with you," said Sanderson.

"The two fire sites and my home are south of Sacramento. So, you'll need to drive south to meet me."

"I'll get you a personal effect of the third victim before you leave today, and I'll contact the other medical examiner's office to see if they have any personal effects in storage. I would presume the family would have picked up the belongings, but then they would have cut the clothes off that didn't burn up in the fire and may still have them," Dr. Galloway said.

Jill caught Maguire flinching at the thought of the victim's clothes being burned off and had a thought.

"Would you like to see victim number four, Detective Maguire? He's still in the cooler."

"No, thanks. Like I said, I'm not sure you have a homicide here. As Detective Rodriguez is handling the impersonation, I'll just leave and get back to the other cases I am working on."

There was silence in the room as the detective left.

"Oh well. That's the detective's loss. This is going to prove to be an interesting case," remarked Agent Sanderson.

Rodriguez gave a slightly puzzled look at the agent and said, "You seem so sure that this case is, in fact, homicide. Yet the evidence seems sparse and circumstantial."

"It's the reputation of Dr. Quint with the FBI, Detective. She also saved the lives of two FBI agents a couple years ago, so we're going to run with her suspicions as she hasn't failed us yet."

Jill hadn't liked the disrespect that she had felt from Maguire, but she also found she didn't like this FBI agent's breezy confidence. Okay, Jill thought, admit it, you're never happy. Either you're being disrespected or sucked up to, and neither approach is making you happy. Sigh.

Jennifer arranged for the security tapes to be sent to Detective Rodriguez. She got the clothing for Jill from victim number three. Jill gave Agent Sanderson directions where they could meet the next day to view the fire scenes again, and the meeting broke up.

CHAPTER 13

*J*ill was about thirty minutes from her home when she got a call. She hit the button on her car's dashboard and said, "This is Jill Quint," as she didn't recognize the number.

"Hi Dr. Quint, this is Detective Mullin."

Jill was so surprised that she found herself pulling off the highway on the upcoming off-ramp. She put the car in park, spending microseconds wondering how she should respond. She decided to play it cool.

"Yes. Did you get the results back on the balloon fragment?"

"I did, and there was evidence of He-4 in abundance."

"That's a helium isotope, and if you inhale enough of it, you will die."

While Jill had the fake cop on the phone, she took Agent Sanderson's card out of her purse and texted him about John Mullin calling her.

His only response was to say he was calling the cellular networks to trace the call. Jill tuned back into the phone call, wondering if she should tell him she knew he wasn't with the CBI.

"Did you get any DNA results on the cigarette butt?"

She then texted the agent, *Should I tell him we know he's a fake cop?*

He replied, *No. See if you can get him to meet us tomorrow at our scheduled time and location.*

"They came back with female DNA."

"Was it a match to the other three victims?" Jill asked the fake cop.

"Don't know yet. What are your next steps on the case?"

I'd like to find out who you are and why you're impersonating an officer, Jill wanted to say. Instead, she said, "That's good information. I'm going back to the other scene tomorrow with Trixie to see if I can find another balloon fragment. You're welcome to join me."

Fake Detective Mullin said, "I'm tied up tomorrow, but let me know if you find any new evidence."

Not until I know who you really are, Jill wanted to yell into the phone.

"Okay, then. Thanks for your help, goodbye."

"Wait! I just wanted to say that you should be sure to keep me informed of any new information."

"So, you think these cases are connected, and they're homicide?"

Jill thought it was bad when she could convince a fake cop of the merits of the four deaths being connected, but couldn't convince the Sacramento Police Detective that it deserved her time. Life wasn't fair.

"I think they are connected, and I think they're homicide. I like your theory about helium."

"Okay then, I'll let you know if I collect any additional information from my searches tomorrow," and Jill punched the disconnect key to end the call. She changed her phone configuration so that the phone detected she was in motion in a car and therefore couldn't answer the phone. She wanted to complete the drive home and think about the fake detective, then she would call Agent Sanderson the moment she reached her home.

The more she thought about the fake detective, the more concerned she became about her personal safety. He had her business card, and with little effort, he could discover where she lived. Her dog liked him, so she offered no defense. Until she had more information on the man, she would stay with Nathan.

She was about to dial him when she remembered that this was Nathan's first day teaching, and he was up north and staying in a hotel tonight. She would text him about staying in his house tonight as it seemed rude to just take over his house in his absence.

Nathan must have not been in class, for he soon responded, *Do I need to be there tonight? Do you want additional protection?*

It was sweet that he would drive all that way to keep her safe. She replied, *No, stay where you are. It's either your house or a hotel. I think we'll have more information on the fake detective tomorrow.*

She reached her home and packed her laptop, overnight clothes, and a few dog items, and she was driving away from her house a short time later. She reached Nathan's house, used her key to get in, and settled in in his kitchen to get some work done. She also had alarms and cameras on her property to know if she was over-reacting or if John Mullin arrived at her house.

Trixie retreated to a soft rug and looked on with disgust when Jill picked Arthur up and set him on her lap to be petted. The cat preened and purred loudly, knowing that it aggravated the dog. She smiled over the thought that some things never changed. She then called Agent Sanderson to see what new information he had.

"Hello, Dr. Quint."

"Call me Jill. Were you able to trace the phone call?"

"Yes, though it wasn't much help. Your caller was in a car on Highway 99 traveling south. We have no road cameras in that area, so short of sending up a helicopter which wouldn't get there before you ended the call, we didn't gain much by tracing the call."

"I hit the record button on my cell phone, so I'll send a copy of our conversation to both you and Detective Rodriguez. It's probably of little value, but I'll close the loop on it. I was a little unnerved by the call, so I'm staying at a friend's house tonight. I have a sophisticated security system watching my house, and I'll know if he tries to find me at home."

"You told him what we were doing tomorrow?"

"I did, but I didn't tell them about the 'we' part. If he shows up, he'll be surprised by your presence. Do you carry a gun?"

"Standard issue for all FBI agents. Are you expecting I'll need it?"

"I don't think so. I didn't sense danger, nor did my dog when we first met him. She's a pretty good judge of character."

"Good to know."

"I'm just completely puzzled. How did he know about this case? How did he figure out the best law enforcement agency to impersonate because it's relatively obscure? You will hear in the recording that the balloon fragment contained helium in the form of He-4, which is the most common type of helium on our planet. He also said he had the cigarette butt analyzed, and it came back with female DNA. Still, he couldn't match it to the previous three cigarette butts' DNA. I wonder if that's all a lie or if he actually had the balloon and the butt analyzed but couldn't match it to the other butts as he didn't have possession of them?"

"Either answer is possible, right?"

"Yes, with a private lab, you could get those results within twenty-four hours. What should I do or say if he calls again?"

"The only thing he doesn't know about this case is that we know he's not representing the California Bureau of Investigation. You're not going to have new information unless you find more evidence at the wildfire scenes tomorrow. So between now and when we're done investigating those wildfire sites, you can pretty much say to him whatever you want. We don't think he's a suspect in these homicides as both the dating site and the cigarette butts suggest a female arsonist murderer. He has some relationship to this case that we haven't figured out yet."

"Okay. I feel a little safer after talking it over with you."

"Did you check with the other counties to see if they have any other male deaths in wildfires that fit the scenario with these four fires?" Agent Sanderson asked.

"I sent an email out to the other counties, and perhaps two-thirds of them responded with a negative. They had no deaths that fit our profile. I'll send out another email to those remaining counties just to close the loop. I looked at the state fire reports for this fire season, and I don't see other fires with the death of just one male."

"Okay, I'll meet you at our designated location tomorrow. I may have a second agent join us from the Fresno office as some of the deaths have been in her territory. Is there anything else I can do for you? Do you feel unsafe?"

"I feel very secure, and my dog and I will see you tomorrow."

After they ended the call, Jill forwarded the recording of the phone call to both the agent and the detective. She provided a longer explanation for the detective. Still, she didn't expect to hear back from him as she gave him all the information that she had.

She had a quiet night at Nathan's house, and no alarms went off at her house. She continued to research the dating app, deciding to focus on men she wouldn't consider dating even if Nathan wasn't in her life. Maybe she could narrow it down to a few targets, and then they could put some resources on the targets. Jill tried to make a long list of the similarities among the four victims. Beyond the ethnicity, age range, and poor spelling, what other qualities could she use to describe the four victims? She printed out their profiles, whom they liked, and who liked them in case their profiles were taken down. After hours spent combing the small details, she didn't have much more than the obvious characteristics. Maybe that was a quality all its own—the men were so shallow that there was nothing there. Jill drank two glasses of wine while first producing the victim profiles and then moving on to potential victims in Shasta County who were on the app. Her final conclusion was that she was glad she was off the market in looking for a mate. Jill didn't need to look any farther than Nathan. She already had her perfect man, and she was grateful because if she stared at that website for much longer, she was sure she would be blind.

CHAPTER 14

$\mathcal{J}$ill, with Trixie in tow, arrived at the rendezvous spot to meet Agent Sanderson. Jill was a little on the early side, and another car pulled into the parking lot close to her. A woman got out and asked, "Are you Dr. Quint?"

"Yes."

"Hi, I'm Agent Jeannie Chan from the Fresno office. Agent Sanderson mentioned you would have a sniffer dog with you. Since you're the only woman with a dog in this parking lot, I deduced with my agent skills that you must be Dr. Quint."

Jill immediately liked anyone who didn't take themselves too seriously, no matter how important their job was.

"Hi Agent Chan, I'm Jill, and this is Trixie."

The agent held her hand out to the dog, and when she got a tail wag, she kneeled to give the dog an ear rub. Jill looked up as she heard the sound of another car approaching and saw that it was Agent Sanderson behind the wheel. They decided to take Jill's car as it had the most room for the dog. Besides, Jill knew the way to the two fire locations and where to park, given that she had already been there before.

As she arrived at the first site, she was tempted to look over the hill and search for the bicycles to see if the hikers were on the trail that day. However, she had two armed agents with her, so she wasn't worried about being surprised by strangers on a hiking trail.

They started walking uphill, and Jill thought about the long recovery time for this small piece of burnt California landscape. She couldn't detect any difference between this trip and the last. The devastation looked the same. There was no sign of life, nor would there be for at least three or four months. First, the area needed rainfall before little green weeds would be the start of the rebirth of this plot of land.

"This makes me mad to see the work of the Burnt Widow. This area is going to look devastated for months."

"Burnt Widow?" asked Agent Sanderson.

"That's my nickname for our arsonist/murderer. I got tired of the word *arsonist* as it seemed like too mild a word to describe her actions. I have a marketing friend, and he couldn't think of a better nickname than the Burnt Widow. It is sort of like the Black Widow, but more suited to this situation."

"I like it. I'll see if we can call this investigation Operation Burnt Widow," said Agent Sanderson.

They were slowly walking uphill, and Jill was carrying the personal effects of the third victim for Trixie to use when they reached the location where the victim was found.

Jill pointed out an area and said, "I don't know exactly where the victim was found. I only have geocoordinates which roughly approximate this area." Jill walked in a circle that covered the area.

She took the item out of the bag and asked the dog to *sniff* and *find*.

They all stood quietly, watching the dog sniff. Jill looked over her shoulder when she heard a piece of brush snap. She stiffened when she saw who was approaching, glad that she had back-up this time.

"Detective Mullin, I'm surprised to see you here," Jill said.

"You said you were going back to the locations to look for more evidence, and that sounded like a good idea. Plus, you have your dog, which is something the CBI doesn't have," replied the detective.

Just then, Trixie focused on something, and Jill forgot about the fake detective as her focus turned toward the dog. She kneeled next to the dog and shifted things around to see if she could locate what had excited Trixie.

"Bingo!" exclaimed Jill, holding up a balloon fragment between the tweezer pinchers and then dropping it into an evidence envelope.

While Jill concentrated on the dog and whatever treasures she found, the two FBI agents had moved close to Detective Mullin. Jill stood up and turned to face the three of them.

Agent Sanderson held up his shield and identified himself, "May I see some identification?"

"Why?" asked Detective Mullin.

"Because I don't know who you are."

Detective Mullin sighed and pulled a business card out of his jacket pocket.

Agent Sanderson looked at it and said, "It's a federal offense to lie to the FBI. Who are you really? We called the CBI, and they never heard of you."

"Really? You must have called the wrong section of my agency."

"So, let me see your shield," said Sanderson.

"We're an undercover unit, so we don't carry shields."

"Agent Chan, please call the CBI, and we'll see if they'll identify Mr. Mullin. Why don't you take a picture of him, Jeannie, and we'll send that to them in case they need it."

Mullin put his hand up to block any picture taking of his face and turned around, clearly intending to flee. He took off at a run, and Jill noted Chan and Sanderson communicate something silently between them and decided not to give chase.

"I'm curious. Why did you decide not to chase him down?" Jill asked.

"I noted the gun in the holster under his arm when he turned to flee. We could have gotten into a shootout over his impersonating an officer. That's likely to have a poor outcome. He's interested in this case, and I will find out who he is eventually. If you didn't have DNA pointing to a female arsonist, I might consider him a suspect. I can't quite figure out his behavior. Did you get his picture?" asked Agent Sanderson.

"How do you know I got a picture?" Jill had found Agent Sanderson friendly and relaxed, but he was far more observant than she had given him credit for.

"You were aiming your camera to take a picture of the balloon fragment, except the angle was wrong, and I realized you were taking a photo of the detective."

"I also got a picture of the balloon fragment. I have a laptop in my backpack that has very sophisticated facial recognition software on it. I can't use it now because there's zero to poor cellular reception in this area. When we drive to the next scene, at some point, I'll pull off the highway and run the picture at that time. I would send you a copy right now, but it won't do you any good as you don't have an Internet connection either."

"Okay. Is there anything else to see here?" asked Agent Chan.

"Yes. I have a theory that Burnt Widow picks locations that have something special about them. With this location, there's a rock structure that's interesting to look at. I was also going to have Trixie do a second round of sniffing to make sure we didn't miss anything. I've already seen the rock structure, but if either or both of you want to view it, it's about ten minutes up that hill," Jill said, pointing to the hill in front of them.

The agents looked at each other, and Agent Sanderson said, "I'll go find your rock formation. Agent Chan will stay with you."

Jill thought about that and said, "That is probably a good idea.

Detective Mullin could return and take the evidence packet from me."

By the time the dog completed her second round of sniffing the crime scene, Agent Sanderson had returned from the hike up the hill.

"Okay, I saw your rock formation. I suppose if you're really into hiking, that's a lovely thing to hike to, and I guess the Burnt Widow chatted up that rock formation to the man she lured here to kill. Did the dog find anything else?"

"No. We're ready to go."

In the back of her mind, Jill wondered if there would be any damage to her vehicle. When she saw her car, she was grateful he hadn't thought to take a knife to all four tires. That would've stalled them from moving on to the next crime scene, as it would've taken a while to get a tow truck out there. The dog and the humans entered the car, and with the agents watching their cell phone reception, about ten minutes later Jill pulled off the road when they had a good cell phone connection.

Jill took a moment to study the picture before uploading it into her friend, Henrik Klein's, facial recognition software program. The program took a little longer than normal and came up with five identities for the mysterious Detective Mullin.

"That's an interesting software program and an interesting outcome—five separate identities. The man has a variety of driver licenses and passport names, but no criminal history, which is either good or bad," said Agent Sanderson.

"What's bad about him having no criminal background?" Jill asked.

"Given that he moves around with five different identities, he may be equally good at hiding his criminal behavior," replied Agent Chan.

"Among these five identities, what's your guess on which one is real?" Jill asked the two agents.

They studied the five profiles again, and not one of them stood out as being more legitimate than the next. The age range fit the man they had met in the woods. The driver's licenses were issued by states on the East Coast.

"If I had my guess, I think the most legitimate identification is the one from Rhode Island. It's the oldest, and I thought I detected a Rhode Island accent," said Agent Chan.

"I'm going to send an email to one of my teammates, who is really good at researching people's backgrounds. I'll give her the five identities with the advice that the first one might be the most legitimate."

"Needless to say, the FBI will do likewise."

Jill pulled back onto the road and continued to the next site. Agent Chan had secured a piece of personal clothing from the medical examiner in the county that performed victim number two's autopsy. After another search by Trixie, more balloon evidence was found among the burnt debris of the wildfire. There was no sighting of Detective Mullin. In the case of both victims, the balloon debris was big enough that Jill could take a sample with her to process at her lab, while the FBI sent a piece to their regional lab for processing.

CHAPTER 15

*J*ill and Trixie arrived back in her vineyard when the temperature gauge was pushing over one-hundred degrees. Given her fear of fire, Jill always tried to block out the wildfires each year, knowing that Nathan or the local sheriff would let her know when a fire was getting close to her land. For her own sanity, she had to keep the thought of the wildfires tucked back in her mind. What was so hard with this case was she had to trample through the scene of a wildfire every couple of days. She also gazed upon victims who met the fate of dying in a fire, which was her greatest fear. She reminded herself that the fire didn't kill them. An arsonist did. She let Trixie loose, where she started her immediate search for squirrels that had dared to enter the vineyard in her absence. Jill took her evidence envelopes and headed for the lab that she'd set up in one of her barns. She paused a moment to think about Detective Mullin. He didn't seem like he would be a threat to Jill despite the number of fake identities. She had her sophisticated alarm system, and she would let it protect her and not run off to Nathan's house.

A short time later, she had an answer as to what was on the balloon fragment. In addition to smoky debris and a type of talcum powder common in latex balloons, she also found evidence of He-4. Now she thought she knew how the victims died. It was due to a lack of oxygen. Still, she wasn't close to identifying the killer. Maybe she could think about suicide with helium, but then, who started the wildfire after the victim died from the helium?

Jill's phone rang, and it was a number she didn't recognize though the area code was close by. It was probably another one of those spam calls.

"Hello."

"This is Melissa Profino. May I speak to Jill Quint?"

"Oh, hi, Melissa. How are you?"

"Did I catch you a good time?"

"Yes, how can I help?"

"You really captured my interest the other day when you spoke about your other job as a forensic pathologist/private investigator. I believe I have a service to offer you, and I would like to become a part of your team."

When Melissa indicated the other day that she wanted to chat more, this was not the conversation Jill envisioned having with her. Still, she was curious.

"What service can you provide that I might need as a forensic pathologist?"

"Before I retired to run the vineyard, I worked in the behavioral science division of LAPD. From what I read about some of your cases, it seems like you might benefit from some behavioral science."

"I would. Some of my cases have touched the FBI, and they'll use behavioral scientists with some cases. However, about a third to half of my cases have been outside of the United States where behavioral science isn't common, so yes, I can use some help. In the current case that I'm involved with, the FBI is assisting, and we haven't had any behavioral analysis. We're pretty far away from identifying our perpetrator. What kind of fee would you charge?"

"How do the rest of your team members get paid?"

"That's just it. We don't get paid for every case. Sometimes we're involved just trying to keep ourselves alive. Other times the client has signed a contract for services, and our vacation accounts increase thanks to client fees. So it's a range of about zero to one-hundred dollars an hour."

"I would agree to work for that. You seem like a trustworthy person, and if you say you're not being paid, I'll believe you."

"That sounds well and good, but it's a little more complicated than that. For example, the Sacramento County crime lab is paying me for autopsy and investigative services up to eighty hours, and I have to document what I do to get payment. I won't be able to charge for behavioral analysis, so I don't have a way to pay you for the current case unless something changes."

"No worries. I just want to keep my skills up and my brain active. If I occasionally get paid, then that's gravy on top. We can use your current case as a way for you to become familiar with my skills. Do you have time to meet this evening? I can't get away from my tasting room before then."

"Sure, why don't you meet me at my vineyard at 6:30? My partner will be here. And he'll make us an excellent meal."

"Sounds like a plan. See you later."

Jill was used to the odd ebb and flow of an investigation. Sometimes she ran out of clues to follow, and other times she and her friends were running for their lives from some killer. It was a job of extremes.

Jill did a quick reference check on Melissa. She was able to verify that she had worked in the named unit of the LAPD. They had been sad to see her go and set up a winery. She then contacted Nathan to tell him about the guest she expected for dinner. Since Melissa was in the wine business, she knew Nathan would enjoy meeting her.

Melissa arrived at the appointed time. Jill gave her a quick tour of both her vineyard operation and her forensic lab. By the time they returned to the house, Nathan had arrived and was working in Jill's kitchen to prepare dinner. He was doing a seafood paella and had a bottle of white wine to pair with their meal.

Jill sat on her sofa with Melissa across from her with a pad of paper. Jill described the case so far with the key points of a female arsonist who was using the dating site Matefinder to find her victims, or so it appeared. She added the speculations about hiking and helium.

"In my years with the LAPD, we had a few arsonists, and I can't think of a single one who was a female. I still have all my textbooks, so I may do a little research and perhaps talk to my fellow professionals. I should be able to provide you with a behavioral analysis by the end of tomorrow. My tasting room isn't open, and so I'll have a lot of time to devote to this."

"Do you have any thoughts on my mysterious fake Detective Mullin?"

"I don't believe he intends to harm you as he had the perfect opportunity when you were visiting the fourth crime scene. My guess about his identity is either he's a relative of one of the victims and seeking justice, or he's an investigator of some sort involved in this case. What I don't know is if he told the truth about the DNA results. You might call and ask."

Jill hit her forehead with the palm of her hand and said, "Duh." She dialed Detective Mullin's number.

"Yes?" said the male voice.

"Hello, it's Jill Quint, and I know you're not a real detective. Did you really send the balloon fragment and cigarette butt from the fourth scene for analysis?"

"Yes, I did. A legitimate lab gave me those results. Are you any closer to knowing who this female is?"

"No. They haven't found a DNA match yet, and I don't think they're going to. What do you know about the Burnt Widow that you aren't telling me?"

"I have no comment."

"Do you intend to harm me?"

"Good God, no. You're too good at your job."

"Good night," Jill said and ended the call.

She had her cell phone on speaker when she made the call.

"What do you think?" Jill asked Melissa. She thought about adding more words to her question, but she didn't want to influence Melissa's answer.

"I think you're safe as you got a gut response from him when you asked if he was a danger to you. Even the best criminal actors don't sound like that so quickly. It was like a knee-jerk response. He seemed offended that you even asked the question. I couldn't tell from your short conversation if I think he's related to one of the victims or to the arsonist, or as you call her, the Burnt Widow."

"On that happy note, dinner is ready," Nathan announced.

The three of them sat down to eat and to discuss the wine industry. Jill had never said Nathan was a wine label designer. When Melissa found out who he was, she pummeled him with design questions. At one point, she went outside to her car and retrieved one of her bottles for his analysis of her label. Jill liked Melissa. She was hard-working, and when presented with the opportunity to learn, she took it and ran with it.

She also enjoyed watching the master at work. Despite being partners for almost three years, she learned something new when he went into wine marketing mode.

After a lengthy discussion, Melissa said, "I should hire you and re-do all of my labels. I have five varietals that I produce."

"I wouldn't necessarily do that. I'm not cheap, and you'll need to earn my fees back in your wine sales. I always advise potential clients that they should make the best possible vintage first before they spend money on marketing. I've not tasted your wines, but do you think they're perfect? Is there anything you could do to make them taste even better?"

"I do think my vintages are as good as humanly possible, but I'd like to have both of you over to my house. I like to cook, and I can pair my wines with a menu of my choosing. When are you both available, and when is it a likely time that we'll need to discuss this case?" Melissa asked.

They discussed their schedules and set a date in two days. Jill was conscious of the fact that the Burnt Widow would strike again in a few days if she stayed on schedule. If she was on schedule and followed her habit, Jill would be driving to Shasta County, which was far enough away that she would likely stay overnight.

"In my experience with the LAPD, many criminals act in a predictable manner. I have no reason to think that you won't be dealing with the new victim soon. If you do get called to a crime scene, give me a call and show me the live video in case it tells me anything about your perpetrator."

"Only one of the four crime scenes has been close enough to a cellular tower for me to have reception. If it is Shasta County, which is even more rural than the other counties I've had victims in, I likely won't have the reception to do a live video call. I will try and film the scene from my car to wherever the victim is found and whatever makes the hike interesting."

CHAPTER 16

Over the next days, Jill received more test results. Not only was the DNA on the fourth cigarette butt female, but it was also from the same female. The FBI was becoming more involved in the case now that it was clear that they had a serial killer on their hands. They had done a multistate search for similar arson cases and, like Jill, came up with nothing. It sounded like the Burnt Widow was evolving into a more dangerous person. Consistent with Jill's belief that these deaths resulted from a hiking date from a match made on Matefinder, it was likely that their suspect was in the same age range as the victims.

Jill also received confirmation that the balloon fragments contained helium particles. They now had their weapon for the last three murders, which was different from the first one. It was a question to ask Melissa as to why the Burnt Widow changed murder weapons. Meanwhile, Jill was feeling the pressure that another hiking date was likely being scheduled, and it would result in a new death. Nathan and Jill were scheduled to go to Melissa's house that evening, which would be a very enjoyable experience that she was looking forward to. At the moment, she needed to think. It was her brain that was usually the most powerful weapon in solving these cases.

She took a pen and paper and a yoga mat and walked out into her vineyard. The air was clear again as her local fire had been extinguished. Maybe if she stretched out and gave the entire case another run-through in her head, she might come up with another angle to explore. Trixie followed her and was puzzled by her settling down on the ground with pen and paper. The dog watched for a moment and then seemed to shrug her dog shoulders as she turned away and went on squirrel patrol.

As usual, the dog's antics amused her. She turned her head down and started writing everything she remembered about the case. It was good to think outside among her vines. Sometimes you just needed a new vantage point while you did your deep thinking.

The one aspect she hadn't explored was how the Burnt Widow moved around the state. She had to believe that the date to go hiking was a second or third meeting for the couple. So how did she stay in an area long enough to date and to learn where her kill site might be? What was her income that allowed her to be on the move and date in so many cities? She wondered if she explored multiple hikes to determine which was the best for her purposes. She thought back to what Jack, the insurance adjuster, said about how a fire spread.

The Burnt Widow would have to find a hiking trail that was rarely used, and had a lot of dry brush to ensure satisfaction with the fire for an arsonist. It needed to be on a hillside where she could light the fire and yet have time to return to her vehicle and leave before firefighters arrived. None of the reports from the firefighters had noted any vehicle leaving the brushfire area. Jill made a note to look again at the fire scenes to see if there was another way to leave the scene other than the way the arsonist might have arrived. If the Burnt Widow did her research to know which way fire vehicles would come from to fight the brushfire, maybe then she knew another way to drive away from the scene.

That was an intriguing thought. It was so intriguing that Jill folded up her yoga mat and returned to the house and the big screen of her desktop computer. She wanted to study the roads around each of the crime scenes. If there was a secondary escape route, that was one more element to add to her list of things the Burnt Widow was looking for when she was searching for the place to do her killing. Maybe if Jill knew that aspect, it might help her narrow what trails the Burnt Widow would use for her next crime scene.

Jill felt that spark of excitement whenever deep thinking about a crime revealed an additional aspect to examine and perhaps gave her additional information about the perpetrator. Maybe it was time to talk to fake Detective Mullin and pick his brain.

She dialed his number and waited for him to answer. She never knew if he would take a call from her.

"Has there been another murder?" was how the fake detective answered his phone.

"Come on, you know better than that. She won't strike until tomorrow, and it will take one to two days to discover the victim."

"So why did you call?"

"Why are you involved in this case? You know impersonating an officer is a criminal act. What's in it for you?"

"I got information out of you, so it was worth that criminal act."

"You're not some random person seeking out random information. You're on this case because you know one of the victims, or you know who the Burnt Widow is."

"Maybe I'm a journalist wanting to write a true-crime novel."

"Yeah, right. I know you're not John Mullin," Jill continued reeling off the other names the facial recognition software had come up with. "So, which name should I go with?"

"You are a very good PI. I'm very impressed. Call me John."

Jill sighed. She wasn't going to get any information out of him that he didn't want to give her.

"I've been thinking about the way the Burnt Widow has been able to move around the state. She has her own vehicle which she drives to the scene, and she's able to move to a new city every week or two. How is she so mobile, and where does her income come from?"

"Why are you asking me? Is that your nickname for her?"

"Yes, I got tired of calling her the arsonist when she is so much more than that. I think you know something about her that you're not telling me. So, answer my question: Do you know how she is so mobile?"

Jill stared at the phone, realizing that John had ended their call. He wasn't going to answer her questions. He was an intriguing part of the puzzle of this case. She wondered if he knew the person behind the Burnt Widow, and if he did, how did he know her identity? At least she had ruffled his feathers by reeling off other names he used. His identity was the FBI's problem, not hers. Still, she kept the phone line open between the two of them in case he let slip some information about their perpetrator.

She turned her attention back to the maps. Maybe she could find a road or business camera on the roads to and from her crime scenes that might carry footage of a car passing by before or after the time of death. She would start with the most recent scene as businesses with cameras might not hold onto video footage for very long.

Using a Google map, she studied the Butte County crime scene roads, then she switched to the satellite view to look at the lay of the land and any businesses close to the murder scene. She wrote a list of businesses to call and was glad she could use the Sacramento Medical Examiner's Office as an excuse to gain footage. She called the receptionist at the ME's office and had her transfer the calls to the businesses so that it would look like the call was legitimate. After identifying herself as an investigator for the ME's office, she would inquire about where any exterior cameras were located and if they had a view of a particular road. Then, when there were useful camera angles, she would request footage for the four hours around the time of death.

The complicated game of telephone tag took up the remainder of Jill's day, and she owed the receptionist some kind of gift for her help keeping Jill connected. After all her conversation gymnastics, she managed to get the footage from four locations. If any of the footage proved helpful, she swore she would go into the Sacramento ME's office the next day just to reduce the phone stress of the situation.

She was just starting to review the tapes when Nathan arrived to drive to Melissa's vineyard. True to her word, she was an excellent chef who wisely paired her vintages with the food she cooked. Nathan had a quick tour of her tasting room on the way over to her house.

"Have you thought about offering gourmet meals with wine as an expansion of your tasting room? You are an excellent cook. Visitors would appreciate the food and any instruction you provide about the pairings. I like what you said when you talked about your wines just now. You would have to hire serving staff, but if you did it as a special request for touring parties, I would think you could manage the food by yourself as long as there were no more than, say, eight people," Nathan suggested. "It would also be a way for your winery to stand out among the endless number of wineries in this area."

"I've been tossing ideas around in my head about some food and wine offerings, but until you described it for me now, I hadn't pictured the idea of a home-cooked meal while wine was discussed. I like it. Can I call you and get your advice when I have a version ready to put forth to the local wine tour companies?"

"I would be happy to help. Since you don't have any sparkling pre-dinner wines, you might make Jill your wine pourer while you cook and talk food. She could bring her Moscato with her and do some cross-selling."

Jill opened her mouth to say something, but she waited to see how Melissa reacted to Nathan's suggestion.

"That's a brilliant idea. I could also expand and find a third winery eventually that served dessert wine or port. I think I would have to make sure people had a ride home or smaller wine glasses, or they would be roaring drunk by the time they were done. Are you game, Jill?"

"Count me in. I'll play wine hostess and help you serve food. Maybe do one or two dinners to see if you like doing them, and they're profitable. If they are a success, you could hire wait staff next or someone to help you plate food. Nathan would tell you I have no skills in the kitchen and if you want to be a success, you had best keep me out of the kitchen."

"You're a chemist, a botanist, and a winemaker. How can you be a bad cook?"

"Her friends pay her to stay out of the kitchen," Nathan said with a smirk.

"That's the way I like it. Seriously, I don't enjoy cooking at all. I know nothing about making food look pretty on a plate. I'm far too happy eating simple fare like a cheeseburger and fries or a pepperoni pizza. Why spend hours slaving in a kitchen? I can pour wine, but if you want your new project to be a success, you'll want me to stay out of the kitchen."

"Okay, I'll go with what you say. I'm sure I'll need to get a food license from the county, which might be the biggest time hurdle and expense. I'll start looking into that tomorrow. Thanks for the great idea, Nathan."

"He's full of ideas on how to expand your business. He's helping a friend who is producing both wine and beer, he's helping another friend expand his winery in Germany, and his label is part of the reason my vintages have sold out each year so far."

"You make me think about changing my wine labels."

"You've got a good artist. Your labels are quirky like you, and I like that in a label. Don't try to look like a serious French wine if that is not who you are as a winemaker."

"More good advice. Thanks," Melissa said.

"Okay, now I want to pick your brain about my case. My Burnt Widow changed murder weapons between her first victim and the next three. What does that say about her?"

Melissa thought about that for a while and replied, "I think that means she's a perfectionist always looking to improve her technique and avoid detection. With the barbiturates, it could have been labeled suicide or a homicide. The next three victims were labeled as accidental deaths from smoke inhalation until you corrected the pathologists, right?"

"Yes, and you're correct that they would still look like accidental deaths not to be researched any further, and given there has been no announcement in the press about this, the Burnt Widow probably thinks that no one is on her trail at the moment."

"Do you have any new thoughts on who my fake Detective John Mullin might be? I called him this afternoon to ask if he knew how the Widow is moving around the state. He had no answer for me and said I was the detective, so I should figure that out. Well, I'm stumped. I wondered if she was retired, but she's too young for that. She must have a digital job that allows her to move around, or maybe a trust fund. That's the only thing I can think of. She needs money to get helium and balloons, and whatever else she takes with her on a hike. She needs money for the vehicle she drives to the fire sites. So, she has some kind of income source."

"That's an interesting question. Several serial killers in this state have held jobs, and several haven't. It seems like a fifty-fifty split. Some start at a young age and escalate their crimes. Those rarely hold jobs, and they tend to serve jail time before finally getting sent to the big house for their serial killer work. That said, so few of them are female. Most female serial killers murder their families—especially their children. There is often a father in the picture, and a lack of income is rarely the cause of their behavior. There have been a few nurses who have killed large numbers of people, and half are male and half female, but employed."

"So, it's possible she could be employed?"

"Yes. She sounds like she is highly intelligent. She uses a dating app and knows about the effects of helium. She's creative enough to find incentives to get couch potatoes to go on a hike with her. The fact that she is killing men probably also gives her a sense of power in addition to the way she feels after watching a brushfire take off. I'm surprised she hasn't accelerated—made her deaths closer together. That shows she has control. Your Burnt Widow can put off the satisfaction of a wildfire because she doesn't want to be caught. As for your fake detective, I'm clueless."

"That's very interesting. I don't know if it gives me any new angle to research who she is and where the Burnt Widow can be found. Work-from-home jobs generally require an internet connection. As long as she spent a certain part of her day within the range of a cellular tower, she could get her work completed. She could be in sales, or computer technology, or a thousand other jobs. Then again, she might be wealthy and have a trust fund available for her use."

When Jill and Nathan returned to her house, she had the footage from the various businesses to look through. It was late, but she needed to know whether she was driving into Sacramento the next day. The three businesses were on one road, and the fourth business security camera footage from another road. She watched the first video footage and slowed it down each time a car entered the frame. It was a slow and tedious process.

Nathan had been watching the footage with her. He asked, "Why don't you use your fancy facial recognition software and have it identify all vehicles that appear in the camera lens. I thought you could set it up to look for inanimate objects?"

"You know I'm brain dead at this time of day, so thank you for thinking of something I should have known. Let me set it up to do just that."

She started by asking the software to find any cars in both locations one and two, three, or four. Over the four hours of the tape, there were exactly two vehicles that matched and were in both sets of security footages.

"Sweetie, you are so smart. I wouldn't have figured that out myself."

"Did you learn anything from the search?"

"Yes, there are exactly two cars that match the location search I was looking for. One is a government vehicle—sheriff or police— and the other is a white truck."

"That's good news! Can you identify the truck or the driver?"

"Wow, you sound like a private detective."

"I have to be dumb and deaf not to have picked up a few techniques from you by now."

"In answer to your question, it's too blurry a picture to see the license plate or who's driving. It is helpful to know that it's a white truck."

"Can you tell who the manufacturer is?"

"I don't see the words on the vehicle, but that front grill looks like a Ford to me."

Nathan studied the picture and nodded his agreement.

She sent an email to Agent Sanderson with the findings from her afternoon search and what she was planning to do the next day from the Sacramento Medical Examiner's Office. It was late, and she didn't expect a reply from the agent tonight. She closed down her computer, looked around to see if she had everything ready to go in the morning, and then dragged Nathan upstairs to her bedroom.

CHAPTER 17

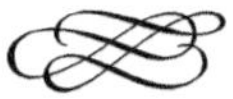

Jill checked her email before heading north to Sacramento. Agent Sanderson was planning to meet her at the medical examiner's office. He was impressed with her idea about business security cameras on the roads near the fire. That was the only new news for Jill. No word from fake Detective Mullin. At some point, she would figure out who he was, and then she hit upon an idea as she was driving. Why not have Marie look up his five aliases to see what she could compile about him? When she arrived in the parking lot at the ME's office, she paused a moment to send off an email to Marie. She was sure if she waited until she walked inside, it would escape her list of things to do.

Just as she started to walk toward the door of the ME's office, Agent Sanderson pulled into the parking lot. Jill noted he had someone else beside him in the car. Great, Jill thought. The more, the merrier. She waited for him to join her on the curb outside the office.

"Good morning Agent Sanderson."

"Hello, Jill Quint. This is another agent from my office, Agent Emily Nome. We've been assigned additional resources and have some new information. Do you know if there is a conference room we could use inside the building?"

"As a matter of fact, there is a conference room—the ME assigned it to me as a temporary office, so step into my office."

"Great."

They went through the process of signing in, and then the two agents followed Jill into the conference room assigned by Jennifer. On the way to the conference room, they met Dr. Galloway who asked Jill and the two agents, "Any news?"

"Actually, there is. Would you like to step inside and join our conversation?" Jill asked.

Dr. Galloway looked at her watch and said, "I'll have to stop by later. I'm due for an autopsy in five minutes, and with what is written on your faces, you have more than five minutes of information for me. I'll circle back when I'm done with my latest gang victim."

"Crips and the Bloods still going at it, huh?" Jill said.

"Yes. Will they never learn?"

With that final comment, she left Jill and the two agents to organize themselves. Jill had returned to the office to make calls representing the ME's office to search for a videotape that might identify her suspect. First, she wanted to hear what the agents had to say.

"We did a national search of brushfire arsons, trying to get a lead on the suspect. However, there are so many arson-related fires in California alone that I couldn't narrow the search. There is no pattern of lone men dying outside of these four known cases. Of course, that means that a lone male dying in a wildfire might be misclassified as accidental death, but short of investigating all of the fire reports, and there are thousands, we haven't found an obvious track record of the arsonist's work before these four cases. There's the other issue too that a past pattern might have been with house fires or some other fire scene."

"I likewise did a search of Washington and Oregon and

reached out to all of the California counties, and I haven't come upon reports that fit this arsonist's M.O.," Jill agreed.

"We spoke with our behavior analysis unit to see if there was anything to gain from their input. They said our arsonist is highly intelligent. We knew that she did catch a break by failing to fall under the radar of law enforcement by successfully staging the brushfires to look like accidental deaths or suicides. They also said she was in her thirties and probably Caucasian."

"So far, none of that is new information. I have a vineyard owner friend who is also a behaviorist. She worked at the LAPD as a behavioral analyst before retiring, and she said the same thing. One thing that no one seems to know is what role our fake Detective Mullin is playing. Did you ask your experts that question?"

"I did. They believe he has a connection to law enforcement. They also said they don't think he has harmful intentions directed at us. They couldn't think of another case containing the odd aspect of our fake Detective Mullin."

"So, what are you working on now?" Jill asked.

"We need to get the DNA report from the outside lab and see if we can match to anyone nationwide. Maybe if we can't find the identity of her directly, we can at least identify a relative of the arsonist's and go from there. We'll also help with the vehicle search."

"Great! I came to the office because calling from my home phone got me nothing. I wasted the time of the receptionist here by having my calls routed through this building. That was painful, so that's why I traveled here today—just for their telephone iden-tification line. I figure the FBI has even more clout, so calling businesses for their videotapes should be even easier. Also, if she's running according to the pattern, we should discover a new victim any day now in Shasta County."

"Sadly, that's true. Let's start making calls. I would say we should move over to the FBI's offices, but we would just waste an hour of your time driving east to Roseville. Our cell phones issued by the bureau say 'FBI,' so that should get us somewhere. I'll have them send us a video to my email address. Then I'll have to fight falling asleep as I watch relentlessly boring videos," said Agent Sanderson.

"Actually, you won't have to watch boring videos. You've seen my facial identity software in use when we identified our fake Detective Mullin. I can also have it search for objects like vehicles. It took twelve hours of video and found the cars I was looking for in under three minutes."

"Jill Quint, you and your technology are something special. We probably have similar technology in use in the FBI, but I bet it takes all sorts of paperwork to use it."

Using Google Earth, they each took one of the other three murder sites. They developed a grid map with the business names of anyone lining the access roads to and from the brushfires. Calling each of the businesses and then waiting to be connected to whoever could give them access and had the technical knowledge to email a piece of security camera footage from a particular date took the remainder of the day.

It confirmed what Jill suspected: their suspect drove a white Ford truck. When some of the security cameras were clear enough to read the license plate, they determined that the suspect's vehicle had different license plates. The white truck appeared on each crime scene's video footage of the roads although it sported different plates on the vehicle each time. Oddly enough, each set of plates belonged to a different white truck, none of which was reported missing. Their suspect must be borrowing the plates for each murder scene and then returning them before the owner noticed. It was further proof that the Burnt Widow was highly intelligent. Also, any footage of the driver revealed various hats and hair, all disguising the face. The hands holding the steering wheel appeared small and light-skinned, which didn't help narrow the pool of suspects. It wasn't proof that the white truck belonged to their suspect, but the recurring appearance of the truck was highly suspect, and it was a crime to switch license plates.

Just as they were getting towards the end of the day, Jill received an email from Marie. She had completed additional research on John Mullin and his many identities and found nothing. The identities exist, but there are no details. Her final comment was, *Perhaps he's a spy or in some secret government organization because darn if I can find anything about him other than his face connected to the name.*

CHAPTER 18

Special Agent Jeff Lawrence had just ended his call to his superiors at the Naval Criminal Investigative Service. He'd spent twenty years doing investigations of rogue Naval personnel. As such, he carried multiple identities given the number of times he'd had to go undercover, including his most recent identity of CBI Detective John Mullin. For over five years, he'd been on the trail of a rogue explosive ordnance disposal specialist by the name of Amanda Moore. The military had trained her as a part of Naval Special Warfare command. She was first in her class at handling explosives. It was only after she was out in the field that the military discovered that her expertise with explosives perfectly suited her arsonist personality.

There began to be reports of excessive "practice," as she called it. She would spend triple the time of anyone else with her title out on the bunkers blowing stuff up. She started a few wildfires in the process with the creativity of the explosives she enjoyed using. She was an expensive trainee as she used so much firepower. However, her superiors were pleased as she improved some approaches with explosives.

Concerns began to surface about a year later after she had

been assigned to a unit. She had a preference for leveling any building they entered, rather than using just enough targeted munitions to smoke out insurgents, which killed all the occupants inside That was rarely the goal of the Navy's use of explosives. Things went from bad to worse when she discovered a flame thrower in the Navy's weapons depot. She began lighting little wildfires all over the base. Access to the flame thrower was removed from her clearance level, but the damage was done. In the explosives workshop, she made a flame thrower with materials in the workshop and was soon out setting fires. The military began to fear sending her out on assignment. Fires, big and little, occurred when Amanda's unit was in the area. She was never seen starting a fire, but it became hard to ignore the coincidence. The breaking point was when one of her fellow soldiers was burned by her suspected actions. The unit spread out on a mission, and Amanda was with the frontline crew assisting with opening doorways for incursions. Once she opened the last doorway, she made to light some fires just to be mean-spirited, and that was when the soldier was burned. During the investigation into what caused the accident, evidence revealed that Amanda was likely starting fires when behind enemy lines, so an investigator secretly shadowed her during the unit's next assignment. There he collected video evidence of her starting fires.

She was arrested, and during the military justice process, a psychiatrist evaluated her and determined she had a psychosis related to fire. He also said she was highly intelligent. In one interview, she spoke with delight about her control over fire, the power of heat, and the sound of flames accelerating through a brushfire. She was tried and convicted in a military court and ordered to serve time. She was a model prisoner and was discharged from the prison and the military. While in the brig near San Diego, she took classes for a post-discharge career. Amanda was granted a mandatory supervised release, but she disappeared and never appeared again for any hearing or follow-up. The military lost track of her and spent about a year trying to find her before her case was relegated to a cold case pile. She was forgotten about until very recently.

A series of fires aboard floating Naval museums on both coasts suggested they were the work of the same arsonist. A shortlist of known civilian and military arsonists pointed to Amanda Moore. A fingerprint aboard one of those ships damaged by fire matched Amanda, yet there was no record of her serving on the ship. It was decommissioned before she was born. Of course, she could have visited the ship as a tourist, but the military had been unable to find her to ask that question.

That was when Jeff Lawrence was assigned the task of finding Amanda and bringing her in for questioning. She would also likely serve additional time in the Brig for violating her parole. That assignment had been five years ago and one of several cases he carried at any given time. It was the most frustrating case he had ever been assigned. Jeff had no idea where she lived or even what name she functioned under. Amanda Moore was an embarrassment to the military three times over. First that they hadn't screened her out as an arsonist before assigning her to work with explosives, second when they hadn't noticed her love affair with fire before she injured one of her fellow servicemen, and third when they trusted her to show up for parole and follow-up. All of those mistakes were made by other people before Jeff got involved.

As a Special Agent, he'd never failed to solve a case before Amanda. He was a civilian member of the Navy, and he'd underestimated her level of intelligence. He shouldn't have as he'd read her psychological profile multiple times, but his confidence in his investigative skills had caused him to underestimate her. On top of her intelligence, the military considered the search for Amanda to be highly confidential. He couldn't reveal his true identity to police or civilians in the search for Ms. Moore. As the years went by, and Jeff was unable to find her location, he vacillated between hate and admiration for her ability to remain undetected. While his superiors were pleased with his investigative skills and how he closed cases, they had been about to move the cold case to a different investigator. That would have been a demerit on his record.

Jeff set up several Google searches to look for evidence of Amanda's work. Every California fire season, he got alerts about fires that might fit her profile. He would run the details down, and there would always be some factor that didn't fit her profile. This year, the thrill of the hunt was on. His Google search led him to a series of fires that fit Amanda. He stole the cigarette butt from the one crime scene and had it matched to her DNA that the military had on file. The military collected DNA from all service members for identification of remains.

Now he was tasked with finding her before the police and FBI. They wanted her back inside the brig to await a trial that would put her away for a long time, and they wanted it done quietly. The military had never informed the serviceman's family that he had been badly injured by a fellow soldier. It would be ugly if that came out a decade later during a civilian criminal trial. The Navy assigned the Director to watch Jeff's efforts to capture Amanda. He wanted her arrested quickly and quietly. He was willing to provide Jeff with any number of military police, if needed, to take her into custody.

That would be all fine and dandy if he knew where she was, but he didn't. The Director was also aware that she had likely killed four civilians so far. That gave the civilians more rights to prosecute her. Instead, he wanted her quietly arrested and tried inside the military. She had applied to the military when she turned eighteen and left the foster care system, so the Director knew they could secure her away from humanity without a family coming to her rescue. This way, the military could hide its poor handling of her case and her personality.

Dr. Jill Quint was both an asset and a liability on the case. She was the one to think about bringing her dog to the crime scene, which had given him the evidence he needed to confirm Amanda's identity. She was also the investigator that figured out the connection to the dating app. However, the downside of all that intelligence was that she also figured out he wasn't who he said he was. She managed to find his other identities and found that he wasn't a detective with the California Bureau of Investigation. Jill knew he had some connection to the case and knew he wouldn't harm her. He'd been lucky at the one crime scene where she was accompanied by the FBI agents. They could have decided to try and detain him, but they hadn't. So where did he go next?

When Amanda was discharged from the military, she received no pension. How was she earning a living? How was she moving around the state to facilitate the various crime scenes? He thought Jill was on the right track with the idea that the hiking date wasn't the first date. She was killing confirmed couch potatoes, and it went against their grain to hike.

She had to stay in the area where she planned to start a wildfire for at least a few days in order to schedule, at a minimum, two dates. She would want to scope out where she wanted to meet her victim and where she wanted his death to occur. She needed to assure herself that no one would come upon her as she was torching an area, so she probably stopped by several times to verify that her target hiking trail was rarely used. He could stop by some of the businesses that lined the road on the way to the kill sites and see if they had video coverage, or he could check out some bars in the towns from which she picked her victims. Maybe if he showed the picture of the victim to a bartender, he might remember the guy and, by extension, Amanda Moore.

Yes, he liked that plan. He'd try the bars first and then the traffic cameras second.

CHAPTER 19

*J*ill was home catching up on the practicalities of life like laundry and paying the bills. She also planned to spend some time reviewing the blueprints for her tasting room. She had set today's date as her final plan approval date. She didn't know why she was so indecisive about the blueprints as she had certainly incorporated every possible thing she liked in tasting rooms she had visited around the world. Jill guessed the problem was she had so many ideas in the tasting room that it no longer felt like hers, which was her own fault.

A half-hour later, having sent her architect her approval of the plans, she leaned back to enjoy the simple pleasure of being on the path to building a tasting room. It was a business success milestone in the winery business. Just when she was at a full-body stretch, her cell phone rang, and she gave a groan that her few seconds of pleasure with the future building were being interrupted.

She picked up the phone, and it said Shasta County Sheriff. This might be the call she was expecting with news of a new fire victim.

"This is Dr. Jill Quint."

"Hi Dr. Quint, this is Vickie Stockdale from the Shasta County Coroner's Office in Redding. I saw the alert you issued for any single male deaths in wildfires, and we just got one in our county."

"Are you doing the autopsy tonight?"

"No, the pathologist is off in the evening. It will be handled tomorrow morning."

"I'd like to be there, but I live south of Sacramento. Would it be possible to delay the autopsy until, say, ten or eleven in the morning?"

There was a pause on the other end of the phone. Clearly, the caller hadn't expected that.

"Let me check with our pathologist, and I'll call you back."

"I know that Shasta County is not in my jurisdiction, but we have had four other deaths across the state matching what you've described. I would also like to bring my dog, who is a trained sniffer dog, to search for similar forensic evidence that we have found at other crime scenes. Is there a place I can leave her indoors while I attend the autopsy?"

"I'll have to check on that, too."

The call ended, and Jill immediately tried to calculate the time it would take to drive to Redding. It looked to be four hours. She would have to be on the road at six or seven. She would pack a bag for both herself and Trixie in case they got stuck overnight, but she hoped to be back in her own bed. A while later, Vickie called back.

"Our pathologist will start the autopsy at eleven, and you'll be able to leave your dog with our receptionist. He's a dog lover, and we're assuming the dog is friendly if it's trained enough to sniff stuff at crime scenes. We'll also accompany you to where we located the body."

"Thanks for your help. By the way, does your victim fit the age and race profile we included in the alert? Was he for the most part, clothed except what burned away, and did you find his parked car nearby?"

"Yes, to all of those questions."

"Okay, I'll see you tomorrow."

As soon as the call ended, she punched in the numbers for Agent Sanderson.

"Hi, Jill."

"Hi, Agent Sanderson. We may have another victim. I'm attending an autopsy tomorrow in Redding for a man who fits our profile."

He sighed and said, "Give me the details."

"It's an active fire scene, but as fire personnel was inspecting the scene, they came across a lone male fitting our profile. I'm bringing my dog with me and attending the autopsy at eleven, and then I'll go out to the location where they found him. The coroner's office is sending an investigator with me."

"I don't need to be there at the start of your autopsy, so I'll meet you at the coroner's office between twelve and one and go with you to the location where the man was found."

"Bring a heavy-duty mask since it's an active fire scene and the air is bad in that area. I'll admit to you that I'm terrified of fire. I don't operate a barbeque, and my house doesn't have a fireplace, so a big wildfire will not be my cup of tea."

"If you want to loan me your dog, you can stay inside the coroner's office, and I'll go with the investigator."

"That's a kind offer. Let me think about that."

They ended their call, and before Jill forgot, she checked the supplies in her autopsy kit in the car. She also packed overnight bags for herself and Trixie in case they were stuck in the area. She hoped to be home as she suspected she would have her usual fire nightmare, and it was better to have it in her own bed where at least Jill recognized her surroundings when she woke up in terror. The car was ready to go and she could head out immediately after breakfast the next morning. She couldn't recall ever visiting the city of Redding. She knew its reputation for hot days and wildfires in any year, but nearly one-hundred-thousand people lived there, so it was a big town. If she got there early enough, she would take Trixie for a walk across the Sundial Bridge, one of the town's most famous landmarks.

When coroner's investigator Vickie Stockdale had called back to confirm Jill's requests, she had also identified their victim. His wallet was in his pocket, though there was no cash inside it. Josh McCloud was their suspected fifth victim. Jill pulled up the dating app Matefinder and found his profile for a suburb of Redding. Like the other victims, his ideal first date was at a bar, and there was no mention of a love of hiking or even visiting wide open spaces. Josh seemed to be a couch potato just like the other victims. Where had the Burnt Widow met him for the first date? Was it possible to hack into his account, or could the FBI get a search warrant to examine the website? She looked at where he lived and where he was found dead. Would the first date have occurred in a bar in his neighborhood? She looked at the map and decided no. There was no point researching the bars of Redding to identify where the two of them might have met for the first date as there were simply too many of them. Maybe he had a credit card charge for a bar, and that would help identify their arsonist. Jill decided this was another FBI assignment. Maybe they could get a subpoena for the website to locate all women who had contacted the victims.

She sent an email to Agent Sanderson with her latest information and suggestions. He hadn't taken offense with her suggestions so far, and hopefully, he wouldn't this time. She stepped away from her computer to call Nathan and chat. With another early morning, she needed an early night for a projected long day. Invariably when they spent the night together, she ended up going to sleep later.

After they chatted, she took one more look at her email before heading upstairs to bed. She smiled when she read the agent's response.

I submitted a request for the Matefinder subpoena yesterday. I'm meeting a judge early tomorrow to discuss before I head to Redding.

Jill loved that the agent was ahead of her in thinking about the various aspects of the case. She wondered how the judge would react to the request. She'd never dealt with judges and subpoenas and didn't know how reasonable they were. They had only circumstantial evidence, but she didn't know what was required to be allowed to dig into a dating app. They had a definite pattern in the five murders and the female DNA.

At some point, she supposed that the FBI would make an announcement of this case to the media. It felt like they had a duty to alert men about agreeing to hikes with female dating prospects. On that last thought, she fell asleep.

CHAPTER 20

Jill's drive north went faster than expected, and she found herself walking Trixie across the Sundial Bridge. As a scientist, she appreciated the structure and the science that it demonstrated. There was hazy smoke from the nearby fire that blocked the sun, so she didn't see the actual sundial in action. The Sacramento River was beautiful, and it was a great way to stretch her legs after the long drive. The heat was rising, and it was already eighty-five degrees as they returned to the car for the drive to the coroner's office.

She arrived at the single-story light olive-green building and parked. It was not an impressive building, but then, the taxpayers hate spending money on coroner's facilities. Who needed a bright shiny building if you were dead? However, forensics had become much more sophisticated lab spaces since the likely date of construction of this building. The coroner was a division of the sheriff's office and likely had to fight for budget resources among other sheriff priorities. In Jill's opinion, the most important feature of a coroner's office was a competent forensic pathologist, and she would know soon if that was what she was dealing with. She decided to leave her autopsy kit in her car as she might get off on the wrong foot if she showed up with supplies in tow. She hooked Trixie's leash and walked to the entrance waiting to be buzzed in.

An employee inside approached to unlock the door. Looking at Trixie, he said, "Ma'am, we don't allow pets in this building."

"Hi, I'm Dr. Jill Quint. I'm here to observe an autopsy with your coroner scheduled for eleven. This is my dog, Trixie who is a trained scent dog. When I scheduled my visit, I was told that someone would watch Trixie indoors while I attend the autopsy. It's too hot to leave her in the car."

"Oh, of course, I'm sorry. I was informed you were coming. I expected a big German Shepherd or a Labrador. I've never seen a Dalmatian used as a trained police dog. I'll be keeping an eye on Trixie while you're inside." The clerk reached out his hand for Trixie to sniff and then gave her a pat once the dog accepted his scent.

Jill brought a bag containing a rug for the dog to lie on while Jill was observing.

"Would you mind if I took her outside for a walk or two?"

"Not at all; she would love that. If you see any squirrels, just tell her 'no,' and she'll resist the urge to yank the leash and chase them. She'll lay quietly on this rug out of your way," Jill said, handing over the leash and the rug to the clerk.

He laid the rug down in the corner of the reception area and released Trixie from her leash.

"Follow me, and I'll take you to Dr. Katz."

Jill followed the clerk through the secure door and into what was clearly the sheriff's crime lab, including the coroner's space. She was given an ugly large white hazmat suit to put on over her street clothes. There appeared to be a bookcase with slots for observers to leave their stuff if they were visiting the autopsy area, so Jill left her purse and shoulder bag in one of the slots before she put on the suit, and then approached the table where a male body was laid out.

"Hi, I'm Dr. Jill Quint. I'm a forensic pathologist and private investigator here on behalf of my role as a consultant to the Sacramento ME's office. We've had a series of deceased single males located within brushfire zones and fear that we have a serial arsonist murderer on the loose in California."

"Hello, Dr. Quint. I'm Dr. Emma Katz, and this is my assistant Vickie Stockdale whom I believe you spoke with yesterday."

Jill nodded at Vickie and said, "Yes, I appreciate your call. The pattern of deaths has so far been every other county going up the state, so I was half expecting a call from your county as the last death was in Butte County."

"Tell me more before we start this autopsy," Dr. Katz requested.

"First, let me ask, did you collect anything from the scene where this victim was found?"

Vickie pulled up something on a computer screen and appeared to scroll down with her mouse.

"No, we just brought the remains in."

"Okay. We've had four male victims, as I mentioned in other wildfires across the state. Each of them has been Caucasian, within a fifteen year age range, with all the locations including a cigarette butt. The most recent three locations also have had remnants of a balloon with helium residue. The first victim had barbiturates and alcohol in his stomach contents. All the victims have profiles on the dating site Matefinder. There has been female DNA located on the cigarette butts."

"Sounds like you have an unusual female serial killer at work here," said Dr. Katz.

"Probably. It appears this female has the means to move around the state, setting up dates with her victims. She then talks these victims, who from their profiles and body composition don't appear to be hikers, into a date where they hike, and then she has them inhale helium. Once they're dead, the Burnt Widow lights a wildfire. Since these cases have occurred in different counties, law enforcement might not have noticed except that a fire insurance investigator noticed the similarities in the first three deaths and reported this to the Sacramento Medical Examiner. The FBI is involved and will be stopping by towards the end of this autopsy to accompany your staff and me out to the wildfire site."

"What are you expecting to find in an autopsy?" asked Dr. Katz.

"I'm expecting that most people would say this victim died from smoke inhalation. I expect the autopsy to show only minor bits of smoke in his lungs as I think he was dead before he had the chance to inhale smoke."

"Okay then, let's see what we have. That's quite a nickname for the perpetrator, the Burnt Widow. It perfectly describes her actions."

An hour later, it was exactly as Jill expected. There were no drugs in the man's system. A toxicology screen showed nothing, though more lab tests were pending. He didn't have enough fire particulate in his nose or lungs for that to have killed him. As usual, he had a wallet on him with no cash, but identification and credit cards. He was a match to the other victims.

As expected, Agent Sanderson joined them toward the end. After introductions were made and identification verified, he listened as the two pathologists discussed their findings.

Jill did an elbow bump with Dr. Katz, thanking her for her help and alertness to the case. They then left the autopsy area and joined Vickie, stopping for Trixie on their way to the Medical Examiner's van that they would take to the fire scene.

As they got closer to where they found this most recent victim, the air got considerably worse.

"The air is really bad here from this fire. We have some respirators in the van. As you can imagine, some scenes have pretty awful smells. Nothing for the dog, though," Vickie said.

"I have a cloth mask made with HEPA filter materials for her. I will have to take her mask off at the crime scene so she can scent for anything possibly belonging to the victim. I'll also have her scent the cigarette brand we have found at all the crime scenes. Do you have the geocoordinates for where the body was located?"

"We do. However, as I picked up the body yesterday, I think I'll be able to remember where the body was found."

"Awesome."

Jill peered through the windshield as they approached a checkpoint guarded by a sheriff's officer. There was very thick smoke in front of them, and Jill felt the pinpricks of terror hovering in the background of her mind. She'd never been this close to what appeared to be a monster fire. Could the fire be traveling this way? Maybe they should turn around and wait a few days before the fire was extinguished. She didn't want to get any closer to the fire.

Vickie rolled her window down, and it appeared the officer knew her and the official van they were riding in.

"Did you get a call for another victim?" he asked through his rebreather mask.

"No, we're going back to the scene where they found the victim to see if we missed any evidence."

Jill was beginning to feel hot. She reached down and grabbed her water bottle, taking a drink. Then she pulled a stick of peppermint gum out of her purse. She could feel the monster close by, and it was closing in on her.

Agent Sanderson was watching her in the front passenger seat and leaned forward to ask, "Do we need to turn around and drop you off somewhere?"

Jill was holding on to her panic by imagining being in Nathan's dojo taking meditative breaths. She would get through this. No way was she sending her dog to a place she was afraid to go. They needed the dog to find any evidence.

"No. I'll make it through this."

The van began moving forward, and Jill closed her eyes and

focused on deep breathing and the thought that the area they were going to had already burned and therefore it couldn't burn again. Soon she found peace, and the panic began to subside.

She opened her eyes when she felt Vickie stop the van and slide the gear shift into park.

The landscape in front of her looked much the same as it did when they stopped at the checkpoint. There were billowing plumes of dark smoke in the distance, the landscape was black, and the air was an orange haze. She felt guilty for wearing a better mask than her dog had, but it was all a moot point as the dog would have to be maskless when she followed her scent to any evidence. They would just have to try and limit their time at the location where the victim was found.

Vickie carried an article of the victim's clothing as well as evidence bags for anything they located. Jill carried Trixie's leash and the pack of cigarettes that matched the brand the Burnt Widow had used at other sites. In a short time, they were at the location where the latest victim was found. This time Jill had the eyewitness of Vickie, who had retrieved the body. That made their search site smaller. She removed Trixie's mask and held out a cigarette to her with the order to find, and the dog went to work. Jill could feel rivets of sweat rolling down her neck and back. She suspected it was the combination of the heat, her anxiety being this close to a major fire, and the weight of the respirator smashing her thick head of hair. She would be a sodden mess when she finally climbed into her car for the journey home.

Sure enough, Trixie found a cigarette butt close to where Vickie indicated the body had lain. She collected that in an evidence bag. Next, they had the dog smell the article of clothing, and she went to work sniffing. When she focused on an area, Jill gently disturbed the burnt brush and soot and came up with a piece of melted latex. Vickie collected that in another evidence bag, and they waited to see if the dog would find anything else. After another search, Trixie came up empty, so Jill reached down to give the dog a reward and, once she was done chewing, slipped the mask back in place. She made her way quickly back to the van, realizing she was completely soaked with sweat. She hoped she didn't smell bad, but with the respirator on, she had little sense of odor other than smoke. Vickie and the agent were a minute behind her, reaching the van. They climbed inside removing their respirators and the dog's mask, and headed back to the coroner's office.

"What's your timeline for processing the cigarette butt and the latex fragment?" Jill asked.

"The lab should be able to give us a result for the latex fragment today. The cigarette butt is a different issue. That might take several weeks."

"I'd like to take it with me and drop it off at the private lab in Sacramento. They have the other butts, and we'll hear within a few days if the DNA is female and if it matches the other butts. I can sign a chain of custody form for you."

"Let me check with my supervisor when we return to the office."

"Okay. Agent Sanderson, where would this case be tried?" Jill asked, not knowing the judicial side of criminal investigations.

"I have no idea. Let's catch the Burnt Widow first, then we'll let the lawyers worry about that."

They continued their drive back to the coroner's office. Jill looked at her watch and realized she would likely get home at a reasonable hour that night. She made a call to Jennifer Galloway to see if she might use their private contract to run Shasta County's DNA test results.

"Tell Dr. Katz she owes me. I'll run it under our contract here," Jennifer said.

That was good news. Jill was just waiting to see if Dr. Katz was interested in having Sacramento County handle the DNA test. She waited outside in the shade with Trixie and spoke to Agent Sanderson while waiting for an answer from Dr. Katz.

"So, what are your next steps?" Jill asked.

"I'll talk it over with my SAC for a second opinion, but I think we have a duty to warn the men in this state who are using Matefinder. That will be a mess. We'll get sued by Matefinder, who will say it is just a coincidence. That could be as it's a popular dating app, but I don't like all five victims having profiles. Yes, they are in the same age range, but the range is somewhat broad. Otherwise, these men have nothing in common except they are all on that website."

"I agree that you need to make a public announcement. One problem also is our killer may go underground once she understands that we're on to her."

"Yes, I thought about waiting on the public announcement until we get Matefinder's data in hopes that it might offer up some clues. However, the clock is ticking, and she'll kill the next person in less than two weeks. She may already have the first date set up. We'll make an announcement at least before the next kill day. She'll strike either Del Norte or Humboldt County if she follows her pattern. Of course, after that, we don't know if she's going to continue north into Oregon or make a U-turn and start going south down the western edge of California."

Vickie exited the coroner's office with a bag in hand. She passed it to Jill for her to drop off at her DNA source. Jill decided she would see if she could drop it at the private company rather than at the Sacramento Coroner's Office. She could make that call on her way south. She gave a sigh of relief as she settled into her car with her dog for the four-hour drive home. It was a relief to drive away from the fire in a well air-conditioned vehicle. She couldn't wait to arrive home and shower. Between the terror of the fire, the heat, and the smoke, she was sure she stank.

CHAPTER 21

The next day Jill received two pieces of information from the DNA company. The latest cigarette butt was used by a female, and all four matched to the same person. That was confirmation that they had a serial killer on their hands. There was simply no other explanation for it. That afternoon she was on a video call with Agent Sanderson and several other FBI agents, including SAC Leticia Ortiz. They were planning a press conference for the next day. They wanted Jill to participate by walking everyone through the similar forensic evidence in all of the cases. They also planned to include the State Fire Chief, who could address how the fires were started.

The hole in their plan was the subpoena for Matefinder. It was a negotiation with a company that was doing its best to protect its subscribers' privacy and support their business needs. They were dragging their feet to the degree they could without being charged with contempt, and at the same time threatening to sue the FBI for severely damaging their reputation as a website to find your future partner and the love of your life. To know that there was a serial killer among their subscribers was not pleasant news.

Still, the FBI decided to take the risk of upsetting the company to potentially save another life. Of course, they had to depend on local media to get the word out as Matefinder wasn't going to help them. They could only hope the next target would hear their message and not go on a hike with the Burnt Widow. It was a catchy name for their killer, which would stick in potential victims' and the public's minds.

This all sounded well and good, but Jill was worried about how the Burnt Widow would react to hearing her story broadcast. Would she leave the state? Would she change her M.O.? Would she go underground and stop killing for a few years? She picked up the phone and called Melissa Profino.

"Hey Jill, how's your case going?"

"That's why I called. The FBI is holding a press conference with a bunch of law enforcement types tomorrow. They have asked me to be the expert who explains the forensic evidence. I'm a little worried about how the Burnt Widow will react. What's your guess?"

"That's a good question. I'm sure she has a compulsion for what she does with the fires and her victims. The Burnt Widow has been successful at least five times. Perhaps she tried some-thing different before settling on the current path, like just wild-fires but not killing males. She's going to find a way to continue fulfilling her desire to start fires. She enjoys the power of watching flames ignite. I don't know why she's killing men on dates. The easy explanation is that she had an unbelievably bad date and decided to fix that in her own way."

"Do you think she'll move to a different state and pursue her serial killer fantasies there? Like Oregon or Washington?"

"Of course, that's a possibility, or she might miss your press conference and do nothing different from what's she's been doing."

"Do you think that might happen?"

"No. I bet she's been monitoring the fires she started and has gotten satisfaction from however many acres have burned. Still, that involves looking stuff up on the state fire website. She could be doing that and still miss the press conference," Melissa remarked.

"But, she might catch the press conference, and then what would she do?"

"Let me think about that question and call you back. I have some ideas, but I want to do a little research on arsonists. I'll have an answer for you within a few hours. Okay?"

"That sounds great. My biggest worry is that by being involved in the press conference tomorrow, I'll put myself in danger from a sociopathic serial killer. That's not the attention I want. I think I'm right to worry."

"Yes, but there are others to kill, like the FBI agents and the fire guy you mentioned. They are almost all men, and I would think she would go for the men first as has been her pattern."

"I hadn't thought of that. I'm a minor player. I'll start worrying when there are attempts made on the men's lives. On that note, can you give me everything you can think of to predict the Burnt Widow's next move?"

"Sure. I'll try to have something for you tonight. That way, if you want to use any information in my analysis for your press conference, you can."

"Thanks. I'll be on the lookout for your email."

Jill wrote a description of the case so she would be ready to talk at the press conference. She also wrote a list of things she planned to withhold as law enforcement liked to hold things back to be used to determine guilt.

She spent a little more time playing around with Matefinder, but she didn't come up with anything new. She was still a little unnerved by her visit to the active fire location yesterday. It made her want to take action to make sure her winery wasn't vulnerable to brushfires. She dug out her drone and planned to fly it around her property to make sure she created a barrier that fire would have a hard time jumping.

After she surveyed, she felt good. There was no brush that could catch on fire. There were patches of greenery everywhere—vineyards, almond trees, and pistachio trees. She also had a road on one side of her property. When she looked at the situation, her house and outbuildings were the most burnable part of her land. They were well protected by a sophisticated security system that she'd put in after her house was bombed in one of her earliest cases. She would have peace of mind that the Burnt Widow wouldn't find much material to ignite on her land.

It was time to switch directions. Jill was planning to spend the night at Nathan's house as they were both back in town, and he liked cooking in his kitchen more than in Jill's. She would take Trixie for a run and then drop by the architect's office to see if she'd worked up a cost estimate for the project. Jill would have to get a loan, and she needed to know how expensive her taste was. She had a ballpark figure, but now that the rubber had hit the road, it was time to get a little more exact.

Later, when she and Nathan were chatting while he cooked, she told him about the press conference.

"It's too bad they want you there to discuss the forensics. If not for that role, you would just be an anonymous forensic pathologist in the background. Now your serial killer has someone to focus on."

"I spoke with Melissa, and her first thought was the Widow would go after men first. That will be my first warning if Agent Sanderson is targeted. So hopefully, I'll be safe. I will admit I was worried enough that I put my drone up in the air to see if the Widow could burn down my vineyard, and I feel confident that she can't as there is mostly green stuff in the area, and I have the security system on my house."

"True, but like some of the psychos you've dealt with in prior cases, she may not be predictable."

"Yes, you're right. I've thought of some other things to research that I want to look at. We haven't looked at helium purchases," Jill said, opening the Google function on her phone.

"Drat."

"What's wrong?" Nathan asked, looking up from his sauté pan.

"There are too many sources for helium," Jill replied, reading something on her phone. "Maybe not. This is interesting. Did you know you can buy a small tank of helium to be used to blow up balloons? Of course, as I read further, this is not the gas that our arsonist is using to murder her victims."

"How do you know that?"

"This tank is eighty percent helium and twenty percent room air. That's not a high enough concentration to cause hypoxemia. The Burnt Widow must be buying industrial helium, which is used for welding or to calibrate analyzers like the ones out in my barn. Still, there are too many of those types of suppliers for me to chase any purchases. She would only need one small tank for all of her kills, but it would need to be pure helium. Sometimes they mix helium with argon, but that mixture is just as deadly as pure helium."

"What other way do you have to track her down?" Nathan asked.

"I guess we need to do more with the white truck. Maybe I'll see if Jo's partner, Jack, can do any photo enhancing to show the vehicle identification number in the front windshield. I must have twenty pictures of the truck where the photos might be enhanced to reveal that information. I just checked a used-car site, and they had three-thousand used white Ford F-150 trucks for sale in California, so it would be hard to narrow that many trucks to our killer."

Jill pulled up the pictures she had and attached them to an email to Jack with a copy to Jo. While Jo, Marie, and Angela helped her with most cases, she hadn't had cause to use Jo's or Angela's skills yet. Jack taught graphic arts at a college in Wisconsin. He would be knowledgeable about any photo enhancement software that she might use for this case.

"On that unhappy note, let's eat."

Jill entered the FBI's Sacramento office and was escorted to a conference room that contained Special Agent in Charge Leticia Ortiz, whom Jill had worked with off and on over the past three years on cases in California and around the world. Agent Ortiz served as a reference for Jill on numerous occasions, which helped her achieve some standing with law enforcement. Agent Sanderson was there and other personnel, including sheriffs' representatives from the other counties and someone from the State Fire Chief's office. The press conference was in two hours, and they were meeting beforehand to discuss what information they would and wouldn't release. Until the meeting, fire representatives hadn't realized the scope of the Burnt Widow, which was the operational name that the FBI was running with. A legal representative discussed the difficulties they were having with Matefinder, which was dragging its feet to comply with the subpoena.

"I suspect they will be hostile once we say their name during the press conference. They will either begin complying with our subpoena or throw up more barriers to our getting the information. At least men will be warned and be on the lookout for the

Burnt Widow," said the attorney. "We have a duty to warn the public that supersedes Matefinder's right to privacy."

"What do you want me to hold back from my explanation of the forensic evidence?" Jill asked.

"Let's stay quiet about the helium in the balloon evidence," Leticia said. "Let's also not mention the 'every other county' pattern, but we'll call her a statewide killer and name the counties and let someone else draw that conclusion."

"Should I mention that the men's profiles suggest that they wouldn't normally enjoy hiking?" Jill asked.

"Yes, I think so. Let's be specific on the commonalities in their profiles. As much as Matefinder is slowing us down, I don't want to decimate their customers. Men who are outside of the profile can relax a little and may choose to have dates in crowded areas for their own protection."

"Have we contacted the sheriffs in Del Norte and Humboldt counties to warn them that she may strike there next?" Jill asked.

"No. Our profiler doesn't have a handle on whether she'll stay in California or go north into Oregon. We just need to make sure that this press conference gets broadcast in the far north of this state. Sacramento has different television stations from Redding, Eureka, and Crescent City, but we've had our media people invite the stations from those areas to this press conference. It's probably rare that they get an invite to something that doesn't appear relevant to their area, so we'll see if they come. If they don't, our media person will send them footage and suggest they broadcast, but we can't do more than that," SAC Ortiz said.

"It's such a sensational story, I can't believe that the television stations wouldn't pick up on it. I bet the story gets national coverage," Jill suggested.

They discussed the conference further and then moved onto other issues with the case. The DNA lab verified that the same female's DNA was on all the butts. Jill mentioned trying to locate the helium source, but there were too many gas sources. She also mentioned the request she made of Jack to see if he could identify the VIN number of the white truck.

"The FBI has its own experts in that area. We'll see what we can do with the photos. Have we located any additional video footage sources from Redding?" Leticia asked Agent Sanderson.

"We're calling around as we speak. One of the routes is through an active fire zone, and it's been evacuated. We can't ask those business owners until they return after the fire is extinguished."

"Do you have an ETA on the end of that fire?" Leticia asked the fire representative.

"At least another week. Can you show me on the map which road you're interested in? Maybe we can let those business owners back in to retrieve the footage. Likely, there's no reason to open their businesses as the air quality is so bad that you don't want to be there. Also, the electricity may be shut off, so they will have no way to power on computer equipment or the internet."

"I'll send a few agents out, and we'll see what we can do," replied Agent Sanderson. "I'd send them with a generator, but that would insult those business owners that may be losing whatever they store in their refrigerators."

The fire representative nodded, "Yeah, I'd be pretty angry if someone showed up with a generator but only wanted to run my computer with it. I'd be angry enough to make you go get a warrant. Then again, people may be nicer on that road than elsewhere in the state."

The agent nodded as he stood up to leave the room and make some calls to his staff.

SAC Ortiz planned to be the mistress of ceremonies for the press conference. She would introduce the case and then have Jill discuss some of the forensic evidence. The fire representative would have a few words about arsonists and the variety of fires associated with these murders. The press conference would end with Agent Sanderson requesting the public's help in identifying the arsonist. He would also issue a warning to those using a dating app to avoid date hikes in areas prone to wildfires until their perpetrator was captured.

As Jill had correctly predicted, the case took off in the media like wildfire, no pun intended, she thought. She was getting calls from national media outlets to the point that she had to turn her phone off. She received emails from her mother in Arizona and her friends in Wisconsin. Her mother had her usual worries about Jill's connection to criminals. Her friends called to tell her how beautiful she looked on television, which brought a smile to Jill's face. You could always count on your girlfriends!

What Jill really wanted to know was, Had their arsonist been listening? If she stuck to her pattern, she might already have lined up her next victim. They might be going on a date to a bar this evening, at which point she would set up a hike that would result in the sixth victim.

The FBI had a meeting in court with the dating app company regarding their subpoena. Jill hoped that the judge would side with the FBI. Then Jill thought of another way she might get at Matefinder's data. What if she performed a twenty-mile radius search of women using the dating app around each victim? Their perpetrator had to be editing her home cities with each victim. Maybe she was setting up a new account with a new name and picture in each city. If she did that, Jill would not find her. However, if she was just changing the city that she now lived in, Jill might be able to see that as a member of the general public using the dating app. Then she thought of another idea. What if she looked at Eureka and Crescent City for any new woman who had just joined the dating app? Suppose their perpetrator was starting new accounts or was editing the home city of an existing account? In that case, Jill should be able to see her profile on Matefinder. By the time she reached her vineyard, she had a couple new avenues to pursue.

CHAPTER 23

*A*manda Moore was working in the living room of her recreational vehicle. She needed to code four additional medical records in order for her to meet her quota for the day. She took a break at one point, standing up and stretching and rubbing her eyes. Someone could go blind, looking at all the boring information in medical records.

She did a quick scroll through her phone, and a word caught her attention.

Arsonist.

She opened the story and started reading it with alarm. Then she began to pace. Then she sat down and spent the next hour looking for both print and video coverage of the story that caught her attention.

She needed to think about this for a while. There was nothing she had to do immediately. She knew that in her heart. They didn't know where she was or even who she was. She would focus on getting her work done, then she could make some decisions about what she was going to do. She returned to reading and coding the medical records in front of her while in the back of her mind her brain was processing options for what she would do next. She finished her work in record time, and just as dusk was setting in, she returned to the story about a "female arsonist murdering men across California."

She took a moment to smile and invisibly pat herself on the back. It had taken five murders for the authorities to realize that something unusual was going on. She watched the press conference multiple times and took notes on what the authorities said so she could decide what they knew about her. She also wanted to think about that plea to the public for their help. She could call the listed telephone number and plant all kinds of false clues. She also needed to cancel her date at a bar with victim number six and think of a new scheme. She really thought she was doing her fellow women a favor by knocking off the worst of the dating world.

She grabbed a beer out of her refrigerator and went outside to think. It was warm and quiet. The campsite where she parked her RV wasn't busy mid-week. There wasn't a lot of ambient light, which gave her the chance to glance at the stars. When she'd been stuck in the brig for so many years, it was glancing at the night sky that she missed most. It was also why she chose to buy an RV rather than rent an apartment. She could live away from people in the great outdoors yet use her satellite connection to earn income.

She wondered if the military was looking for her. She'd never shown up for any parole meeting, never wanted to be in contact with the military ever again. What did they care if she didn't show up for parole meetings? She decided they weren't looking for her. The FBI was concerning, though. She didn't want them searching for her as she thought they probably had more tools than the military to find someone like her.

She looked down at the list of information they had about her. She wondered if that was all they knew or were they holding back additional information. Had they figured out how she was killing her victims? They knew all the victims used the Matefinder website. Did they think the dating app was a coincidence, or did they know it was the source of her victims? Maybe she should find another dating website and keep up the same process. The question was, how many men caught the news of the Burnt Widow? She smiled at that. She rather liked the nickname they gave her.

She could also head north to Oregon and start over with the same process, although she had to think that with the FBI involved, they would be watching for that. She looked over at the fire pit that was powered by propane gas. She could spend hours staring into the pit's flames, but it was too warm a night to light it.

As she sat staring at the stars, she made up her mind about what to do. She liked her current mission as she learned to call it from the military. Tomorrow she would pack up and head south. She needed to get lost in California's big cities as she would be much harder to detect. She thought she was working under the radar screen by sticking to the smaller eastern cities of the Golden State, but now she could see that someone had been alerted by the similarities among her victims.

She would switch dating sites, but she liked the helium balloon method for killing. Actually, she would stay off the dating sites and just pick up random men from bars. She didn't need a dating app to find these men. They were easy enough to find by just focusing on bars. Not only did she have an industrial tank of helium, but Amanda also had a miniature tank with a mask that she carried in her backpack. That way, once her victim passed out from the lack of oxygen, she would hold a mask over their face with more helium to make sure they were dead. It was a very gentle way to die, and she was proud of thinking about it. A search of her RV would find both tanks and the mask, likely with DNA evidence of her victims. She would get a new mask and melt the current one as soon as she started another fire.

Maybe she should get some metal so she could pretend to be a sculpture artist, and thus, that was her excuse for having the helium tanks. It was best to cover her bases any way she could. Then another idea came to mind. She could solve two problems with one solution and disrupt the investigation. She was excited by her idea and returned to the RV to start digging on her laptop. An hour later, she had a new plan to execute on her way south.

CHAPTER 24

Jill was having dinner with Nathan at the same time that Amanda Moore was completing the work of her day job. Both women's minds were hard at work. One was trying to find Amanda, while the other was trying to hide her actions from law enforcement.

"You looked great on television today. Serious, smart, and sexy. You reminded me of some extremely competent medical examiner from a TV sitcom."

"Thanks, Sweetie. That's music to my ears, especially the serious and smart attributes. I want the public to be concerned and worried, but I want them to feel like we are doing everything possible to find this killer. We didn't release all the information we have on the Burnt Widow, but in holding something back, I also hope we didn't look like we were bumbling through the investigation."

"I'm biased about the case as I know more about it than the average citizen. However, my assistant Lily watched the news, and she said, "They were lucky to have you on the case." So there you have it—a spontaneous reaction from your average citizen."

"As though Lily ever has anything bad to say about anyone."

"True, but she could have said nothing, so take that as a positive sign."

Jill's phone beeped with an unusual ringtone. She had set it to notify her with a different sound if Jack sent her an email.

She glanced down and opened his email. He had tried all kinds of techniques to read the numbers just inside the windshield of the white truck in the pictures. He was able to read ten of the seventeen digits. Jill surmised that there was a supercomputer somewhere that could take all the VIN numbers and figure out which were trucks. Of course, the Burnt Widow might repaint her truck, or she might have had it repainted after she registered it. The license plates represented a multitude of states, not just California. She thanked Jack and then reached out to SAC Ortiz. She heard the FBI had a supercomputer that would have to do this calculation—ten of seventeen digits known against 274 million vehicles in the United States. If the Burnt Widow purchased her truck in Mexico, Jill was screwed at figuring out who the owner was. She sent off an email to Leticia and then returned to her conversation with Nathan.

"Let's move on to a more interesting subject for you. I purchased grape juice from a supplier. It's the Nero d'Avola grape that I planted and should be able to harvest next year. I played with fermenting in an oak barrel and a bourbon barrel. I also tried double fermenting in a third barrel to make a sparkling red. Let me know what you think," Jill said, producing three bottles labeled A, B, C. Given the different cork, it was clear which wine was the sparkling wine.

"Are you trying to invent a new wine varietal?" Nathan asked.

"I suppose I am. Bottle C is like a Lambrusco, but it's made with a different grape."

"That may be hard to market if no one knows what to compare it to."

"I'm sure you'll create a divine label that will sell the wine."

"Have you tasted any of these wines?"

"No. It's going to be a surprise to me, too. Hopefully, a pleasant surprise."

"Wow, I've never tasted one of your failures."

"With any luck tonight, you won't taste one. Maybe they will all be delicious and perfect."

"Has that ever happened?"

"No," Jill said with a laugh. "At least one of these bottles will be a failure and perhaps all three."

"Okay, I've never been on the ground floor of someone's creation before."

"If they taste bad, you'll never want to participate this early again."

"Ah well, let's get to it. Let's start with C as I can't remember the last time I tasted Lambrusco. I'm expecting carbonated Welch's grape juice."

"Hopefully, it won't be that bad," Jill said, pouring them both a sample. She laid out some water crackers to cleanse their palates with after tasting each wine.

Both Nathan and Jill held their glasses up to the light and swirled them. Then they took a sniff. Then each took a sip, then Jill drank her entire glass.

"I love bottle C. It's fizzy and sweet and tastes like red wine. You will have to make a special label for this varietal. It's going to sell as well as my Moscato."

"I guess that means you like your sparkling red."

"Come on, admit this is better than any Lambrusco that you've tasted. Wouldn't this pair well with a steak?"

"I'm not one to like sparkling wines, but I'll admit this is good. I think you'll fill a niche market with this wine. Now you have to come up with an amazing name."

"How about Nero's Extravagance? It is a name that fits the Roman emperor Nero. Although. . . he wasn't a good man, so I probably shouldn't name a wine after him."

"If you indeed bottle this, you're going to have trouble with whatever name you pick. I've never quite thought about this problem before. Maybe you can trademark it and become the sole source for it. You'll need to contact an attorney to understand your intellectual property rights."

"Wow, that's a lot to think about. Thank you, I will contact an attorney. So far, you and I are the only two people who have tasted this miracle sparkling wine."

"Okay, let's move on to bottle A. I want to see if this wine tastes anything like the Nero d'Avola wines we drank in Sicily."

Jill poured them each a glass, and they repeated the process.

"Nathan, meet Jill's failure #1, better known as bottle A. This wine is so full of tannins, I can't taste most of the flavors this grape is famous for."

She dumped the remainder of the wine in her glass down the sink. Nathan followed her lead, glad he didn't have to tell her that her wine was awful.

"Okay, it's on to bottle B. Will the burned inside of a bourbon barrel make this awful wine any better?"

She opened the bottle and poured them each a sample, and they went through the winetasting regimen.

"Okay, this is a wee bit better. I might be able to work with the fermentation to create a palatable wine."

"I wouldn't do that. Your bottle C was so good, why not use all of your grapes for a sparkling wine? It's either that or you hope that your own grapes taste better than the grape juice you purchased."

"You have given me a lot to think about. I love the idea of a sparkling red wine, but I have to agree with you that coming up with a proper name will be half the battle. It's been nice to worry about grapes instead of the Burnt Widow."

"Your grapes are your future and are a statement as to the mark you'll make in the wine industry. You'll catch the Burnt Widow in a few days, and she'll be someone else's problem."

"Speaking of which, here's an email from SAC Ortiz. They do

have a supercomputer in the FBI, and it's going to work on the possible VIN numbers for the Burnt Widow's truck. Maybe we'll know who she is by tomorrow morning. Let's hope so. She's been smart so far, and if she caught the news conference today, she might be changing her modus operandi."

"Did you ever get anything from Matefinder?" Nathan asked.

"No, they claimed they don't keep a record of who contacts whom on their website. I already searched the victims' profiles and found no common females by picture or name. I don't know enough about software to know if what they said was true, but it appears to be a dead end."

Jill reverted to talking about the possibilities with her new sparkling red wine, and that topic consumed them for the remainder of the night. Jill was woken by a call at three in the morning from SAC Ortiz.

CHAPTER 25

"Hello, Leticia," Jill said after checking the caller identification and punching the green button on her phone to connect.

"Sorry to reach you in the middle of the night, but I just received notification that Agent Sanderson died in a house fire about an hour ago."

That sentence had Jill sitting up in bed as Nathan turned the bedside light on.

"What happened? How can I help?"

"The agent lived alone in a small house in a city called Lincoln about ten miles away from our office in Roseville. The fire department responded to calls from his neighbor that the house was on fire. The fire was too fierce to enter the structure when they arrived, but once the fire was contained, they confirmed a male occupant, who they assume is the owner, Agent Sanderson. His body is on the way to the Sacramento Coroner."

"Wow, is there a special fire investigator on the scene? One who could link this house fire to wildfires started by the Burnt Widow?"

"We're sending our own investigators and crime scene experts in addition to whatever city resources investigate the fire."

"Any sign of anything suspicious?"

"Too early to tell. I'm requesting that you participate in Brandon's autopsy. You see things that others don't."

"I'll have to check with the Sacramento Coroner's Office. I'm not their employee, but perhaps they would allow me to observe while their pathologist performs the post-mortem exam. I'll call and see if I can get an answer."

"If they give you any grief, I'll hire you as the FBI's expert and demand that you be there."

"Leticia, I used to work in that office, and they have been gracious and cooperative with me personally. They hired me for eighty hours of work for the Burnt Widow case. I don't expect any barriers from them as his death is so obviously related to the other cases. I'll let you know what we find."

"Thank you, Jill. Agent Sanderson is the first agent I've lost in the line of duty. I owe him and his family everything possible to find this arsonist."

"We don't know the cases are connected yet. Perhaps the house fire was truly accidental."

"It wasn't. I'm sure it was the Burnt Widow."

"Okay, well, let me make some calls to Sacramento and see what I can find out."

Jill sighed and looked over at Nathan, saying, "Agent Sanderson died in a house fire about an hour ago. He was the lead agent that I've been working with the last few days. He made the pitch on camera to call with any details about the Burnt Widow. Crap. Now, SAC Leticia Ortiz wants me to be there for the autopsy. So, I've got to call the coroner's office and see what they're up to and if they'll let me observe."

He nodded and said, "I'm glad you spent the night here, and I think you should continue to stay here at night until she's caught. Is there anything I can do to help?"

"Thanks, no. I'm wide awake now. I'll go grab some coffee as I make calls. I'll leave Trixie here, and I'll probably head out at five."

Jill looked at her watch and thought about the ninety-minute drive to the medical examiner's office and the fact that it was now a quarter after three in the morning. She needed to contact Dr. Jennifer Galloway, but she hated waking her. She left Nathan's bed and went into the living room as there was no sense keeping him awake.

She texted Jennifer, first testing the waters.

Are you awake? It's Jill.

Of course. I'm called whenever a member of law enforcement is brought here. It's a big deal and very emotional. I'm sure you remember. What's up?

Jill thought of the honor guard that formed around any fallen officer and knew how tough it was inside and outside.

I'll call you.

After the greeting was out of the way, Jill asked, "Would it be possible for me to observe the autopsy for Agent Sanderson?"

"I'll have to ask the FBI as it's their agent."

"SAC Leticia Ortiz called me a few minutes ago to inform me about Agent Sanderson's death and asked me to perform the autopsy. She's the Special Agent in Charge for Northern California. I don't need to perform it. Just observe it."

"Ah, I wondered how you knew. You have some amazing acquaintances. I thought you might be an insomniac watching the news and figured the death was related to the arsonist."

"No, I was asleep until the agent called. I'll text you Leticia's number to call and verify that they want me there. Should I hit the road now? I'm about ninety minutes away, closer to two hours if I take the time to dress and brew some coffee."

"Yes, leave now. I'll start the autopsy when you arrive. I've not known you ever to lie, but a law enforcement autopsy is fraught with emotions, so I'm going to call your FBI person."

"Thanks, Jennifer."

Jill texted Leticia with the information that she would be attending the autopsy for Agent Sanderson and to expect a call from Dr. Jennifer Galloway.

Then she took a quick shower, dressed, grabbed a croissant from Nathan's kitchen counter and a go-cup of coffee, and she was out the door. She needed to get gas before she hit the freeway, so Jill knew she would be closer to the two hours estimate that she'd given Jennifer.

When she got to the medical examiner's office, she found the building surrounded by law enforcement officers. Agent Sanderson would be guarded until his burial, as was the tradition. Despite working with him on this case, she knew very little about him. He hadn't mentioned a wife or children.

To get into the parking lot, she had to wait while a call was made to Jennifer Galloway to approve her presence. She was given permission to park and kept her head down and away from the news media vans lining the street as she entered the building. Just inside the door, she took a minute to gather herself. She thought she had found her balance in the drive thinking about what evidence she would look for during the autopsy, but now she had to take great gulps of air and wipe away tears, and she thought of the agent's kindness when she was freaking out at the fire scene. She was glad no one was in the stairwell to watch her lose control.

She was thankful she hadn't put on any make-up as she would have cried it off in the past three minutes. She straightened up and searched and found her stiff upper lip needed for the next two hours. She entered the locker room to change into scrubs and grabbed a protective gown to put over the scrubs. She then entered the autopsy suite and almost lost it again when she saw Leticia Ortiz standing at attention, on guard duty, for Agent Sanderson.

Jennifer Galloway looked up, seemingly relieved that Jill

arrived to share some of the strain of the situation, and then she began dictating to the overhead microphone.

"Dr. Jennifer Galloway, Medical Examiner, Dr. Jill Quint, forensic pathologist, Special Agent in Charge, FBI, Leticia Ortiz, and Forensic Pathology Assistant Robert Keller are in attendance."

Jennifer proceeded with the autopsy, a process Jill had done herself over a thousand times. They accessed the x-rays and lab work taken as soon as the agent's remains had arrived at the office. His blood showed an unusually high content of carbon monoxide. That was a common lab finding for victims of fires. Still, the pathologists noted that for follow-up when they evaluated the heart and lungs. His skin had the pinkness of someone with carbon monoxide poisoning. When they got to the lungs, Jill and Jennifer looked at each other as Jill said, "He wasn't breathing when the fire started. My guess is she pumped carbon monoxide into the bedroom. That would be why he didn't escape the fire. He was already dead."

"Agent Sanderson was murdered?" asked SAC Ortiz.

"Probably, we can rule out suicide as there was no evidence of a source of carbon monoxide near his remains. What we can't rule out is the source of the carbon monoxide. It might be a broken gas stove, gas heater, or gas water heater. We'll have to talk to the fire department about that."

"Could the Burnt Widow send gas into an open window in a house? Would she gain enough concentration to kill someone?"

"Probably. The evidence would be gone as soon as the fire started. The agent could have inhaled it in his sleep without ever waking up again," Jill replied, then asked a question. "Why start the fire? He was already dead. Was she burning up some evidence? Was it her signature event—always start a fire?"

"I don't know. That's a question for the behaviorists, which I'll get them to think about today once I'm done here."

Jennifer was quietly finishing the autopsy while the two women watched and spoke.

"Special Agent in Charge Ortiz, we're done here, and I'll issue a report that says the agent died from carbon monoxide poisoning, either by accident or by homicide, pending the fire department's findings. Is there a family I should talk to?" Dr. Galloway asked.

"I checked our records, and the surprising answer is no. Agent Sanderson was all alone in this world. He grew up in foster care, did a stint in the military, and then joined the FBI. I'll ask the Sacramento office if they know if he was dating anyone so we can include him or her in the funeral planning."

"Okay, then our forensic pathology assistant will close everything up, and you're free to move his remains. We can certainly store the remains here pending any funeral preparations you now have to plan."

"Thank you, Drs. Quint and Galloway, for handling this autopsy. It was important to me that he had the best forensic experts to take care of him."

Jill nodded, wondering briefly where she should go next. She had no work to do in this building, but she also wanted to comfort Leticia in private. She thought she knew her well enough to at least give her a hug. In the end, she waved goodbye to Jennifer and headed to the locker room to change.

Leticia followed her inside and asked, "Would you come with me to the fire scene? I'm meeting the fire inspector there."

"Sure, but let me give you a hug first. You never want to lose an agent, and Brandon Sanderson was a good agent and a kind man."

After the awkward hug, Leticia stepped back and said, "Thank you. I'm holding it together, but barely. When I get home tonight, I'm going to hug my husband and teenagers and spend time telling them that I'm so happy they are in my life."

"If you don't find any significant others, I'd be happy to help you plan the funeral since I spent some time working with Agent

Sanderson. I have a story to tell about his kindness that would resonate well at his funeral."

"Thank you, Jill. I may take you up on that."

"You may want to have additional security around your house. The Burnt Widow could be going after anyone who spoke at the press conference yesterday. I'm staying with Nathan until she's apprehended. My vineyard has a ton of security, but I'm not going to make it easy for her."

"Good point. I have good security on my house, but I may move the family into the FBI building until she's captured. Here's the address of Agent Sanderson's house in Roseville. I'll meet you there," Leticia said, handing Jill a piece of paper with an address on it.

Jill planned to stop at a coffee shop she knew to be in the ME's neighborhood. She needed a hit of caffeine, given the lack of sleep and the stressful autopsy. She was about to leave when she asked Leticia, "Hey, I'm going to hit a coffee shop on the way. Do you want me to bring anything for you?"

"Actually, I'll follow you out of the parking lot to your coffee shop. I need some caffeine and some food."

Twenty minutes later, they each had their coffee made-to-order and some food to keep them going, and they headed for the freeway. Jill followed Leticia's car for a while and then decided she needed to speed. Leticia was a far more conservative driver than Jill, and it was taking the fun out of driving for her.

Jill arrived at the address, and the street was still cluttered with fire and police vehicles. Jill parked outside of their zone and leaned against her car, sipping her coffee, waiting for Leticia to appear. She figured she could hop into her car for the ride through all the official people. A short time later, the agent's car came to a halt next to Jill, and she opened the door to get in.

"You drive like a bat out of hell."

"It's a habit. I consider the posted speed limits to be suggestions."

"Do you have a lot of speeding tickets? I don't remember seeing that when I first researched your background."

"I don't. I have an eyeball in the back of my head scanning for cops, and so far, it's saved me from getting ticketed."

The car had moved forward to where a cop was standing, and Leticia flashed her badge. She was waved closer and told where she could park. Jill looked at a house that had sustained serious fire damage. The houses in this neighborhood were separated by green lawns, so the fire hadn't spread to the houses on either side of Agent Sanderson's.

Leticia approached the fire inspector and the cop waiting for her on the front lawn with Jill on her heels.

She held out her credentials and said, "Leticia Ortiz, Special Agent in Charge, FBI, Northern California, and this is Dr. Jill Quint, a forensic pathologist and private investigator. What can you tell us about this house fire that killed my agent? We've just come from his autopsy. We know that he didn't die from smoke inhalation or burns from this fire. Rather, he died from carbon monoxide poisoning. So did this house fire start from a bad gas appliance, or was the fire intentional?"

This wasn't Leticia's usual way of speaking to law enforcement representatives. Jill thought it must be the weight of the agent's death and perhaps the lack of sleep.

CHAPTER 26

"We just concluded before you arrived that this fire was intentionally set. There are accelerants that were used for the fire. However, more importantly, we have footage on a neighbor's doorbell security camera of a female arsonist spreading accelerant. Perhaps this is the same female that is starting fires across the state," said the fire inspector.

"Can you tell which accelerant was used?" Jill asked.

"We got lucky there, and she is one smart arsonist. She's lighting fires with isopropyl alcohol."

"How did you determine that? If I recall from my chemistry class, isopropyl alcohol burns fast and leaves no residue."

"The arsonist spilled some into the grass away from the house, and it didn't burn. Our lab just identified it."

"Could she use that for brushfires? I don't believe we've identified how she is lighting fires."

"It very well could be. The arsonist's latest fire has been burning for several days. The alcohol may have dissipated by now."

"I have a sniffer dog. Would she be able to detect such a chemical?"

"I don't know. I'm not a dog expert. Cal-Fire does have an accelerant dog that you might request for your other scenes."

"What else did you find here?" asked SAC Ortiz.

"We received a 911 call from one of the neighbors and responded within three minutes. Upon arrival, the house was engulfed, and the neighbor indicated a single male lived there. Fire personnel were able to enter and found an unresponsive male in his bed. He was carried outside, and resuscitation was attempted. Paramedics continued CPR, and he was pronounced dead at the hospital. Fire personnel continued to work on extinguishing the fire, and approximately two hours after the arrival of the fire squadron, we considered the fire extinguished. Due to a report of the suspicious behavior, we've spent more time at this scene collecting evidence and involving our colleagues in the Roseville Police."

"I'd like to walk through the house if it is safe, and I'd like to interview a few of the neighbors. He appears to have no next of kin, so I'll be searching for the presence of another person in his life."

The fire inspector looked at the shoes that both women were wearing and said, "It's not safe for you to enter in those shoes. There is debris everywhere, and you might step on nails, glass, or other objects that will puncture your shoes. There's a shoe store a few blocks away that sells safety shoes if you want to go there and buy something to wear."

"I have combat boots in my trunk. I'll change into them and come back to you," Leticia said.

"I don't have proper shoes, and I'm not sure I can be of use here, so I'll walk back to my car unless you need me for something, Leticia," Jill said.

"Actually, I would appreciate your investigative skills when I speak with the neighbors and look at the door video. Would you mind waiting while I search for evidence of someone else in Agent Sanderson's life?"

"I'd be happy to help. I'll just grab a seat at the curb and read my email while you're searching."

"Thanks, Jill."

Jill did exactly as she said and found a shady part of the street curb to sit on while the fire inspector and the detective accompanied Leticia inside the house.

She sent Nathan a text with what she was up to. Then she called Melissa Profino to get her analysis of the arsonist's latest actions.

"Hi, Jill."

"Hi Melissa, do you have time to talk at the moment?" Jill was trying to remember her tasting room schedule.

"I do for the next hour. What's up?"

Jill explained about the press conference and the agent's death.

"So you want to know if she's coming after you and the other FBI agent?"

"Yes. Did the Burnt Widow choose Agent Sanderson because he was the only male at the press conference, or is she taking us on one at a time?"

"I think she has a plan in her head that she is following. I think her ego was getting a boost with each fire and kill that she made. She felt very assured that her killing spree hadn't come to the notice of law enforcement. When she found out through a press conference that you were aware of her activities, that became quite a blow to her ego, and so she's striking out. I think she'll come after you and your FBI friend. She may also switch dating sights and change states or head to Southern California, figuring that the news of her killing her dates hasn't followed her there. However, I would think she would come after you ladies first before she sets up shop in the south."

"Okay, both the agent and I are moving out of our homes. I'm staying with Nathan, and the agent is moving her family into the FBI building until we capture her. Do you think she'll get a little more reckless now that she's been discovered?"

"I do. She was reckless in killing the agent. She left evidence of her accelerant and her presence. If she had thought this through, she would have been a little more careful."

"Okay. Thanks for your telephone evaluation. I know the FBI has experts, but you know the full story, and you're an expert too. Is there anything I can do for you?"

"Stay safe and invite me into your cases. So far, this one is really interesting. Are they all like this?"

"I've had my share of weird cases and international cases. Imagine trying to figure out what a Russian or an Italian is going to do. Got to run. I'm needed for something here," Jill said as she saw Leticia exit the house carrying something.

She stood up and waited for the agent to approach. She was carrying something in her hand.

"I found a girlfriend. I'm going to give her a call, then we'll visit the neighbors, okay?"

Jill nodded. She was glad she wasn't making that call. She resumed reading her email and looked up when she saw Leticia approaching again.

"That was awful. They were engaged. I'm glad he had someone in his life. We'll include her in planning the funeral. Let's grab Roseville Detective Paul Long and go talk with these neighbors."

Jill accompanied them on the interviews but didn't learn anything that Leticia and Detective Long hadn't also learned. She watched the doorbell camera in fascination. It reminded her of one of her early cases when she watched her property's cameras as a sniper entered her vineyard. There was nothing like seeing the murderer for the first time.

The Burnt Widow appeared to be of average height and weight. She was dressed all in black, but a few glimpses of her face revealed her to be light-skinned. Her hair was covered, and she carried a backpack. There was no camera angle on the side of the agent's house, so they couldn't always see what she was doing. Jill guessed that she carried a carbon monoxide tank and blew the air into the bedroom where the agent was sleeping. Then she reappeared on camera and appeared to be spreading the accelerant. She had a couple of what appeared to be two-liter soda bottles that she used to spread the accelerant. Then she tossed a match and took off down the street and then off-camera.

"We need to see who else has house cameras on the outside that might have captured her or her vehicle," Jill said.

Jill said the words they were all thinking as they turned to walk down the street. An hour later, they had collected additional footage. Best of all, the arsonist stumbled in the dark, raising her face briefly as she caught her balance.

"I have my laptop with me in the car. It has special facial recognition software on it. If you'll email that video footage, we may have an identity for our arsonist," Jill said before heading back to her car with the others trailing her. She powered up the laptop and looked for the email from the detective. She sent the video through the software. There were a few identities for her picture. The reliability of the facial match to the various names varied from seventy to ninety-eight percent. They read the information about each identity. The one with the lowest match was with a woman named Amanda Moore. The picture was taken some twelve years ago upon her entry to Navy boot camp. The lower match was typical with an older photo.

"Does it say what she did for the military?" asked Detective Long.

Jill did a different search and replied, "Amanda Moore trained as a munitions expert. However, she was dishonorably discharged. That's rare, and I would guess even rarer in a female member of the military."

"It is. I served. It was less than one percent. I would guess she served time in a military prison. I wonder what she did?"

"She was an arsonist in the military and appears to be an arsonist now. She was trained in an area of the military that might be the worst possible choice for someone with arsonist tendencies. I bet she was first in her class at blowing things up. It would have given her satisfaction like nothing else."

"How about any of the other identities? Let's go over those," SAC Ortiz said. "I see she has a California driver's license under the name Allison Montgomery that is current. I think that is likely the name she is using today since she's keeping it current. Jill, can you find that name in the Matefinder app?"

"I'll go one better and see if I can find a match on the Matefinder website to her driver's license photo."

She had the software search all the United States for matches, but there was none.

"Perhaps Amanda removed her profile after the press conference yesterday. I'll search for any of her names just to be sure."

Again, there was no match.

"Where to next?" Jill asked.

There was silence as everyone thought about the next steps. Leticia had never planned a funeral and was worried about her first effort being a consequential law enforcement funeral. The Roseville detective seemed to be having a hard time finding footing with the women. They went off in their own direction, and he was left trailing. Jill had a thought cross her mind.

"Detective Long, I gave you an overview of the arsonist's actions, but I left one thing out. There was a fake detective involved in this case. Like Amanda Moore, he has several identities. Detective Aaron Rodriguez of the Sacramento Sheriff's Department was supposed to be following up on his impersonation of an officer from the CBI. Maybe he has a connection to the military."

Detective Long just stood there looking at her, blinking. He clearly didn't follow how she'd drawn her conclusion with so little explanation.

"Let me back up," she said.

"Yes, please do. I'm not sure I heard this part of the story about this weird case," SAC Ortiz said.

"A man presented a business card to the Sacramento ME's office that said he was Detective John Mullin, and he arranged to meet me at the third wildfire crime scene. I was going there with my dog Trixie, a trained scent dog, to look for evidence. The dog found a cigarette butt and a piece of a latex balloon, which Detective Mullin allegedly took with him to the state. I called the lab with a question only to discover that they had no detective by his name. When Agent Sanderson and Agent Chan accompanied me to the first two wildfire sites to look for more evidence, John Mullin appeared at one of them as I had let him know that I was going there. When he saw the two agents upon arrival, he took off at a run, away from the site. I have his cell phone number, and I've talked with him a couple of times. I managed to take a picture of him and ran it through my software, and he came back with multiple identities. He did tell me that the evidence he collected from the site did indeed go to a crime lab for analysis. The cigarette butt contained female DNA and the latex balloon contained remnants of He-4, which is the most common form of helium. He acts like a member of law enforcement. He has investigative skills. Given her dishonorable discharge from the military, perhaps he is a member of the military police looking for her?"

The Detective and SAC Ortiz stared at her during her explanation, and there was silence when she finished. To be fair, she knew a lot more about this case than the two of them and had time to process her reaction to Detective John Mullin.

Finally, SAC Ortiz spoke, "You might be onto something there, Jill. I'm going to have to call up my chain of command to see if we can connect him to the military and to understand what happened to cause her to be dishonorably discharged."

The detective had also been thinking. "My brother is a captain in the Navy. I'll see if he can find any information on Amanda Moore. Let me write down those dates. Since your software is so nifty, why don't you search for her profile among some of the other dating apps?"

"That's a good idea. Unfortunately, that means setting up my profile on each website as that's the fastest way to search. A court order for the website takes at least a day. If I'm not needed here, I'll head home and begin that painful dating site search process."

"Sounds like we all have our next steps. I'm heading over to Agent Sanderson's fiancée's house. Please send me any new information as soon as you get it."

"Remember, I have a two-hour drive in front of me, so it will be a while before you hear back from me," Jill said. Looking at the detective, she said, "I live in the Central Valley."

Jill reached Nathan's house in the early afternoon after stopping by her house to gather things for an extended stay at Nathan's. Fortunately, there was no pressing work in her vineyard. She hoped to have this case ended in under a week, especially now that they had somewhat of an identity of the arsonist. First, she needed a nap. Getting up at three in the morning, followed by the emotion of Agent Sanderson's death, had left her sleepy and depressed. Just before she drifted off to sleep, she had another idea on how to find the Burnt Widow.

CHAPTER 27

*N*early an hour later, she woke up from her nap, groggy because she had slept deeply, but not ready to sleep anymore. Jill had showered before she climbed into bed for her nap as she felt she was full of bad scents despite the fact she hadn't stepped inside Agent Sanderson's house. Falling asleep with long wet hair meant that it was still wet. She took a moment to dress and dry her hair and then checked on Trixie. Nathan had no appointments that day, which left Trixie the opportunity to run at will around his property. Arthur tended to curl up outside Nathan's office, preventing the dog from going near the cat's owner. She checked outside, and all was right in the animal kingdom.

She settled onto Nathan's sofa and began researching the dating sites. She started with the largest first. She would set up a profile entering the minimum amount of information, then she would go to work looking for Amanda Moore or for a match of her picture. Three hours later, she sent an email to SAC Ortiz and the Roseville Detective that she had not located their suspect on any dating site. She asked if there was any word on the VIN number. She was waiting for a reply when Nathan walked in with Trixie and Arthur at his heels.

He leaned down to kiss her and then asked, "How's the investigation going?"

"It's incredibly sad to perform or observe an autopsy on someone you know and like. Agent Sanderson was poisoned by carbon monoxide, which killed him, and then his house was lit on fire. Poor SAC Ortiz has to plan a law enforcement funeral with the agent's fiancée. Glad I'm not in her shoes."

"Do you want me to attend the funeral with you?"

"That's kind of you. It's a very sad and symbolic funeral. As we speak, he has officers guarding his remains. I will be speaking at the funeral, so I'd appreciate you coming if only to carry Kleenex for me. I'll warn you, I'm a crier at an event like this."

"Really, I don't think I've ever seen you so overcome such that you would need a box of tissues."

"When I got to the ME's office in Sacramento this morning, I had to have a quick cry in private in the stairwell before I changed into my autopsy scrubs. The honor guard was outside, and it was very sad and solemn."

"I'm sorry," he said, sitting next to her and hugging her.

"Thanks."

Nathan sensed she was ready to move beyond thinking about the sad circumstance of the agent's death.

"So, what's the latest on this case? Do you have dates set up on the Freshlove website?" he asked, looking at her computer screen.

"No, I was just going through to make sure I deleted all the profiles I set up on all these dating sites. We identified the arsonist and . . ."

"You did? That's big news," Nathan said, cutting Jill's explanation off.

"Yes, I suppose it is good news. We found multiple identities, and our perp served in the military where she was a munitions expert."

"Really? The military trained an arsonist in how to blow things up? Isn't that a little like asking a raging alcoholic to stock the shelves of the Officers' Club bar? Just keeping my thinking in military metaphors."

Jill smiled at his explanation.

"Yes, after we identified her, I called Melissa a second time just to get her opinion of whether the job in the military could have made her an arsonist, and she said "it didn't." She entered the service as an arsonist. It's not like if the military determines you would make a good sniper because of your hand and eye coordination, that you'll be a serial killer because of the training."

"Okay. So, her superiors just didn't notice that she was an arsonist before they sent her to training."

"Exactly. She was dishonorably discharged and changed her name. We were wondering if she did something with fire inside the military to earn her that dishonorable discharge."

"Maybe she harmed a fellow serviceman or woman. I think the military has its own prison system."

"It does. It has its own justice system. You get sent to prison after you've been court-martialed. I was reading up on it, and you get court-martialed for violating the Uniform Code of Military Justice. A military lawyer represents you in court, and five officers serve as a panel. A judge presides over the trial. It was only put into place after World War II, which I found surprising. I would have thought it at least dated back to the Civil War."

"That's more than I know. I never served in the military, and I'm generally a law-abiding citizen. If they ever ask that question on 'Jeopardy,' I know the answer now."

Jill looked up into Nathan's face and said, "See all the random facts you learn by dating me? In the past couple of weeks, you learned that most bodies don't burn in wildfires and about court-martialing. On top of that, I invented a new varietal of wine."

"Babe, you're a woman of infinite and weird qualities. Just put an end to this arsonist, so I don't have to worry about your wine suddenly gaining a smoky flavor."

"That's a good point. Maybe I should move my wine barrels off the property."

"You have a sprinkler system in your barrel room, and if you move the barrels, you'll disturb them and potentially damage the vintage."

"True."

"Besides, didn't you sell your property ownership to a corporation licensed off-shore?"

"I did. The records show that the property was sold by me to a corporation. I also bought one acre in Kern County with a three-hundred square foot hunting shack on it. My name is on the title. Let someone burn down that house."

"I don't recall you telling me about that."

"The attorney who handled the change of ownership for this land recommended that, and he found the one acre property for me. I've only seen a picture of it, but I've never been there. I think it cost me like six thousand dollars for my peace of mind. Seemed like a good idea."

"So what are you going to do as you become increasingly popular in the wine world? Your name and Quixotic Winery will be easily Google searchable, and people will find you."

"I know. I've been thinking about that. I was thinking for the winery business, I should run under my middle name and last name. No mention of being a doctor, or I could do my first and middle name. So it will either be winery owner *Jill Isabella* or *Isabella Quint.* What do you think?"

"I think you should be Jill Isabella. It's a plausible last name, whereas Quint is unusual, and any bad criminal will assume it's you or a relative. With the first choice, people in the wine industry will still call you by your first name. Isabella flows well with Quixotic too. Both words are Spanish in origin, I believe."

"All good points. Meet Jill Isabella, vineyard owner. Now I'll have to work with you and my lawyers to cement this new name and make Jill Quint disappear."

Jill heard her computer ping the sound of an incoming email. She gave the screen a brief glance to see if it was from Ortiz. She confirmed that it was indeed her name that she saw in the sender line.

Nathan patted her knee and walked to his kitchen, knowing that her attention was focused on the email and whatever findings it contained. He wasn't sure what he wanted to cook, and he needed to stare at the ingredients he had on hand before he made his mind up. If nothing caught his interest, he would see if Jill wanted to dine out.

Jill clicked on SAC Ortiz's email; and it noted that the FBI supercomputer had massaged all of the potential VIN numbers matched against white Ford F-150 trucks. It came up with a match to a gray Ford F-150 truck with a particular VIN. None of the other combinations yielded the vehicle make and model in the picture. Leticia had already run the VIN number through the California DMV and got a match to a gray truck licensed to the name that Amanda used on her driver's license—Allison Montgomery. She must have had the truck repainted at some point after she had it licensed. She was smart in that the variety of license plates that she used all related to a white truck, not gray.

Jill thought of something else and asked if Allison Montgomery had any other vehicles licensed to her name. She asked SAC Ortiz to look that up for her and then set aside the laptop to see what Nathan was up to.

"What's for dinner?"

"How do enchiladas sound?"

"Homemade?" Jill asked, knowing that whatever Nathan cooked, it would be delicious.

"Of course. You can help me."

"Awesome."

Jill followed his lead, and soon they had a pan of rolled-up tortillas filled with chicken, black beans, and Mexican cheese. A tasty red sauce and jack cheese were sprinkled on top, and the pan was placed into the oven to bake.

"That was easy. I bet I could do that myself."

"Yes, you could. It would require that you shop for the ingredients, though."

"That always the sticking point, isn't it?"

"Face it, you are the queen of a refrigerator filled with condiments. You don't actually have any food inside."

"I do that so I can enjoy your great cooking. Why shop for stuff that will rot before I can use it?"

"You do have a point. Would you like wine with your enchiladas, or I could make margaritas."

"I'll take a margarita. It's all about getting the food—booze pairing right."

They settled on the couch for some mindless home improvement television while their dinner baked. Jill had an eye on her laptop and reached for it when she saw another email arrive from SAC Ortiz.

She read the email and nodded to herself.

"What?" asked Nathan.

"I figured out how she is moving around the state. She pulls a recreational trailer behind the truck. That would allow her to spend days in different areas by leaving the RV in a park. Now the question is, how does she pay for that RV? Time to ask Jo to do a little work on this case."

"Will she be able to find anything?"

"She might. It's strange the amount of financial information that is posted on the internet."

"How about the address she has on her driver's license? Does that mean anything?"

Jill banged her forehead in disgust.

"Gosh, why didn't I think of that? What a rotten investigator I am."

"Don't you think that Leticia Ortiz looked it up or the detective?"

"Yes, they should have done that. Let me take a look at Google Earth for the address."

Jill used the satellite view of Google Earth and determined the address on the driver's license was a vacant lot. She then looked up the ownership of the lot and discovered it was owned by Allison. However, as the land was empty at the moment and in the middle of nowhere in the California desert, she decided that was a dead end, and that was probably why SAC Ortiz and Detective Long hadn't mentioned it to her.

She sent off an email to Jo but didn't expect an answer back that night. There was no more work she could think to do on the case that evening. It was time to focus on Nathan and the lovely night ahead of them.

CHAPTER 28

Jill awoke the next morning, thinking about what she planned to do next. They were closing in on the Burnt Widow. So far, she hadn't had any alarms go off at her vineyard. So maybe she wasn't on the radar of the arsonist. Jo hadn't responded yet with any financial news. There was nothing new from the detective or SAC Ortiz either. She expected that a Be On the Lookout, or BOLO, had been issued for the truck. If the Burnt Widow was wise, she would have her truck painted again—back to its original gray. That way she would avoid any BOLO alerts.

Jill debated where she should open one of the Cal-Trans road cameras and see if she could monitor one herself with her software. She opened the camera on Highway 80, which was the freeway next to Roseville. There were so many cars whizzing by that she concluded it was a lost cause.

She sent Leticia and Detective Long an email asking if either had requested the highway cameras look for the white truck. She got a quick response that they couldn't do that. There were far too many pick-up trucks on the road for highway cameras to analyze them, which confirmed her earlier decision not to watch the vehicles on I-80. Jill received an email from Jennifer Galloway with lab results for Agent Sanderson. No surprises, and all the evidence confirmed that he died from carbon monoxide.

She saw an email from Jo. Maybe that would contain new information. She opened it and read. It had new information, but not anything that would help them find the Burnt Widow. Jo had found her name associated with a company that performed medical record coding. An Allison Montgomery was listed as one of their coders. Now they knew the source of her income and how she could work remotely. Jill mused she was a regular law-abiding citizen working hard for her wages. She might be supplementing her income from her victims, though, because none of them had been found with any cash.

Now at least they had a picture of how she was moving around the state. She towed an RV and worked from the trailer to earn a regular income. Jill wondered what had set the woman off. Had she been starting wildfires all along and decided to add killing into the mix as a change of pace? Another reason to call Melissa and get her analysis. It was still relatively early, so she would wait until a decent hour to call her and get her opinion.

Jill turned back to the dating sites and thought about what she wanted to do there, or was there another pattern they could follow? What if Jill looked at all the fires across the state? Could she guess which fires the Burnt Widow might have started, and would that give them a path that she was traveling? It was worth a try. She started with the Cal-Fire website as they ended up handling most of the wildfires. City fire departments also battled brushfires within their cities, but she seemed to stay out of the big cities. Perhaps there were too many people around to see her start fires, or perhaps the fire couldn't grow into a big blaze, or perhaps she was worried that bigger cities also had many more random cameras throughout.

Jill started with the dates that they knew the Burnt Widow was suspected of killing their victims. She looked at other fires in those areas around the dates and looked for a pattern. Two hours later, she decided she couldn't assign any fires to their suspect. The reports weren't detailed enough, and there was no single detail that she could associate with fires started by their arsonist.

She dialed Melissa to get another consult.

"Hey Melissa, can you chat for a few minutes?"

"Yes, I've had my coffee, so I'm awake, and my tasting room won't open for several hours. What's up?"

"I was thinking about our arsonist. What set her off on this killing spree? There are enough fires across the state that she could have been at work for years starting small fires. What happened that caused her to add homicide to the fire mix?"

"That's a good question. Since we don't have a full profile on her and I've not interviewed her, I can't vouch for my reasoning. There is mental illness that has made her an arsonist, and so her mind is working in ways beyond the usual healthy brain. I should add that since you started work on this case, I've done a little more research into arsonists. Throughout the past one-hundred and fifty years, arsonists have been viewed as either criminal or mentally ill. Most behaviorists believe that arsonists have a compulsion to start fires. There is some treatment for compulsive disorders. With some arsonists, psychotherapy helps; and others are tried on a course of anti-depressants. Maybe your suspect stopped therapy or ran out of medication. Sexual abuse can be a trigger, so if your arsonist had a bad date or was a victim of sexual violence, that might have set her off."

"So, she likely has no endgame in mind with starting fires other than not to be caught?"

"Yes. She might pull back from her current course if she gets medication or therapy restarted. Otherwise, her compulsion is going to continue to be a problem for her. The monster has been let out of the bag, and she can't put it back in without some external help. Does that help?"

"It makes sense. When I was in medical school and doing clinical rotations, I avoided psych rotations to the degree I could and still graduate. I have the wrong temperament for that profession. In my career as a medical examiner, I didn't need to understand psychiatry. Rather, I needed to understand the difference between a self-inflicted death and an accidental death, and that's probably the closest I got to delving into my patients' psyche."

"Yes, you did select the right clinical track to stay as far away from psych as you could. It's impossible to psychoanalyze the dead. You should expect her to continue to set fires. Remember she has a compulsion driving her, and the fact that she went after Agent Sanderson suggests that she is not slowing down anytime soon."

"Okay, I think I have it. Thank you. How's the planning going for your gourmet meal and wine tasting event?"

Melissa and Jill continued to talk through her plans to offer a gourmet meal and then ended the call.

Maybe it was time to call her fake Detective Mullin and see what he was up to and boldly ask him if he had any relation to the military. She weighed the positives and negatives of alerting him to anything in the investigation, and then she decided to go for it. She dialed his number.

"Yes, Dr. Quint?"

"Hello fake Detective John Mullin; whoops, you told me to call you John."

"Do I detect a note of sarcasm in your voice?"

"You do. Tell me, are you connected to the military?"

"No," came the quick response. There was something in his voice that said he wasn't telling the truth.

"We know who our suspect is and that she served in the Navy, and that she was dishonorably discharged. I assume that's because you folks didn't know she was an arsonist when you signed her up to be a munitions expert. Imagine the military training an arsonist to blow stuff up. That's what I call a match made in heaven, no pun intended."

"Hello?" Jill couldn't believe he had ended their call. She looked at her phone just to make sure she was hung up on. She debated whether to call him back and see if it was a mistake, but she knew it wasn't, or he would have called her back by now.

Sometimes she made a move in a case to agitate a reaction, and she sure got one with "John." Jill was sure he was connected to the military given his reaction to Jill's statements and his overall bearing. However, it was hard to separate the look and behavior of someone in the military from someone in law enforcement.

She should probably confess to Leticia what she had just done in case it came up in the conversations between the FBI and the military. She sent her an email describing her conversation. She couldn't think of anything more to work on with the case, so she packed Trixie into her car and returned to her vineyard. It was too early to do extensive pruning of her vines. Instead, she walked the property looking at where an arsonist might do damage to her property. She also visited her barn, cellar, and house, checking out the alarm and smoke detection systems. There was nothing more she could do to prepare to defend her property if the Burnt Widow turned her attention toward Jill. A couple hours later, she returned to Nathan's house, restless, but without any new information to process for this case.

CHAPTER 29

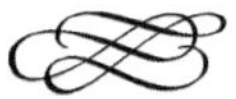

*A*fter the call from Dr. Jill Quint, Jeff Lawrence was in a bit of a panic. He had been impressed with her investigative skills, but still, he was surprised that they had identified Amanda Moore as the arsonist. It was time to talk with the Director again about cooperating with the civilians. They knew who she was and some of the details of what she'd done while in the military. Now she had killed an FBI agent, and the stakes were much higher for the Navy to work with the FBI. He had made an appointment to speak with his commander by phone as soon as he abruptly ended the phone call with Dr. Quint. He was about to connect for his phone appointment.

"Sir, thank you for agreeing to my call."

"Special Agent Lawrence, what news do you have for me?"

"Sir, I just received a disturbing call from the forensic pathologist and private investigator working on this case. She said that she and the FBI know their arson suspect has a military background and was dishonorably discharged."

There was silence on the other end as his superior thought about his next steps. Then he heard a sigh.

"We seem to be getting hit by all sides on the issue of this arsonist. Naval Command received a request for a meeting to discuss the arsonist, making direct reference to her military service."

"What do you want to do, Sir?"

"I wanted to keep her misdeeds hidden, but the civilians seem to be faster than the military in bringing this case to a conclusion."

"Sir, the civilians have different weapons than the military, and they aren't trying to keep a lid on the case. However, she did kill an FBI agent. At least we haven't lost any additional service members, thanks to her."

"Yet. As long as she is on the loose, she could still cause more damage."

"That's correct, Sir. In fact, there have been a series of recent brushfires at our bases in Northern California. She was quietly living out her life and starting the occasional fire, but now her behavior is changing, and she's become extremely dangerous. I would recommend that you meet with the civilians. Perhaps in San Diego, so it's on your turf, Sir."

"Of course, Agent Lawrence," said the Director, who then ended the phone call.

Jeff had called his superior for direction, and he hadn't received any that he could see as he recounted their conversation. What should he do next? He had his answer an hour later when he received a command to be at the Director's office just before five that afternoon for a meeting with the FBI and his office. He felt better after receiving that message. That likely meant he wasn't being fired today. He called base operations at Lemoore Field to see if they had any planes flying to San Diego in time for his meeting. If not, he would look to the Fresno airport to get him south on time. It was nearly a six-hour drive, and he couldn't make it by car in time. He wondered if Jill Quint was going to be invited to attend.

He found she was invited when she approached the gate he was waiting in for the flight to San Diego.

"Hmmm, I think my guess was correct; you *are* associated with the military, and now we're going to the same meeting regarding the Burnt Widow. It's a small world, Detective John Mullin."

"Actually, I'm Special Agent Jeff Lawrence of the Naval Criminal Investigative Service, or as they say on TV, NCIS."

"Sometimes, during an investigation, you have to shake a few trees to see what falls out. My call to you was exactly that."

"Yeah, well, it worked. Naval Command was also being pressured by the FBI, so the case was being worked on from both ends."

"Good. Are you going to tell me about Amanda Moore or Allison Montgomery?"

"Who is Allison?"

"Your sources aren't the best, are they? Amanda changed her name to Allison. She has a California driver's license issued in the name Allison Montgomery."

"I knew you were a good investigator from the moment I met you at that murder site. When this case is over and if I still have a job as an investigator with the Navy, I'd like to have you come present this case and any other interesting cases you solved to our other investigators."

"I can do that. Someday you might also invite the FBI. Even though we're civilians, our methods would work in the military, I think."

"Probably. Service members have fewer rights and less privacy compared to their civilian counterparts. So tell me what you know about Amanda."

"And spoil your surprise in the meeting later?"

"Remember, the capture of Amanda Moore is a cold case. She served her time in a military brig and was released for parole but never showed up. I've been hunting her for at least seven years."

"Ouch. Did the DNA on the cigarette butt match her DNA?"

"How would I know that?"

"Doesn't the military keep records on all members, including a DNA sample?"

"Yes, we do, and we did get a match for Amanda for the butt."

"You didn't think to tell me? I can't see how it would have prevented Agent Sanderson's death or the death of the man in Shasta County, but why wouldn't you tell us?"

"You'll find out at the meeting we're going to. Is the FBI coming as well, or are they sending you as their spokesperson?"

"Special Agent in Charge Leticia Ortiz is based in San Francisco. She's flying out of SFO to San Diego. I live in the Central Valley, so Fresno is the closest airport. Where are you stationed?"

"Lemoore Naval Air Station. We have all the Pacific fighter squadrons based there. There are about fifty-five thousand people on the base between military, civilians, students, and families. I tried to catch a flight to San Diego from the base, but I missed the last one out today."

"What lousy luck you have to find me on the same flight."

"I don't think so. As I said, I admire your intelligence and investigative skills."

They got called to board, so there was no more conversation until after they landed and settled in a taxi together.

"Will this taxi get into the base? Or will we be walking from the front gate?" Jill asked, looking at her watch. They had about forty-five minutes to reach their destination on time, and she wasn't sure how far away the base was.

"My ID will get us past the front gate. This taxi company has been approved by the military."

"So, we should arrive on time."

"Yes, with time to spare. Was SAC Ortiz landing before or after you?"

"Before. There are many more flights between San Francisco and San Diego than fly out of Fresno. She should be there before us by about fifteen minutes."

Indeed, when they arrived at the front gate, Leticia was

waiting there as her transport wasn't allowed on the base, but she could ride along with Lawrence and Quint when they arrived. It was a crowded back seat with the three adults. Jill performed introductions.

SAC Ortiz quipped, "So you're fake Detective John Mullin. It's going to be an interesting conversation. I believe the military has a lot of explaining to do."

"We're not answerable to civilians."

"When one of your members goes on a civilian killing spree, then I think you are. Besides, doesn't NCIS report outside of the Naval command structure directory to the Secretary of the Navy?"

"Ex-member. She hasn't been a part of the military for many years."

"Yes, but you were on the lookout for her and have been for quite some time. If she was an ex-member, why the interest in her?"

"I'll let my superior explain it all to you." With that non-starter, their conversation ended.

Jill couldn't remember being on many military bases. She supposed as a child she had visited one for an airshow or something. She'd never had a desire to serve and frankly thought she would be lousy at following rules simply because someone of higher rank ordered her to do so. Still, she was grateful that people chose to serve, and she knew several of her fellow physicians had paid for their medical education with a stint in the military or the reserves.

Special Agent Lawrence directed the cabbie to a building. He apparently knew his way around this base even though he was stationed elsewhere. Most of the buildings looked similar—square or rectangular government looking buildings in off-white with clay tile roofs. In the distance, she caught sight of some big ships and lots of people in various uniforms.

The cabbie stopped in front of a building that said Pacific Fleet Command, and they got out.

Jill thought of several things to say but wisely kept her mouth shut as she was on unfamiliar ground. She didn't know the rules the military played by, so she would keep quiet until she figured that out.

The two women followed Special Agent Lawrence inside the building and to a conference room. They all took a seat and were offered bottled water. Shortly, an older, Hispanic man arrived in a business suit.

"Hello, I'm Director Gomez, NCIS Pacific Fleet."

Jill stuck out her hand and said, "Dr. Jill Quint, a forensic pathologist and private investigator."

Leticia followed with, "Leticia Ortiz, Special Agent in Charge, Northern California, FBI."

The Director looked at Jeff Lawrence, who replied, "Dr. Quint and I shared a plane ride and a taxi here, and we picked up Special Agent in Charge Ortiz at the front gate, so we already know each other."

"Ah. I believe we have a mutual problem by the name Amanda Moore."

"Yes. She murdered one of my agents early yesterday. By the way, she's changed her name to Allison Montgomery. That was after she murdered five civilians. Why is the Navy searching for her?"

"We're about to have a confidential conversation that I expect to stay in this room as I'll be talking about a service member's personnel file."

"That may be true, but the FBI is searching for a serial killer. Her crimes outside the military likely outweigh anything she did inside the military. I think she served her time in the brig and was released, and then you lost her to follow-up. Is that correct?"

"Yes. That is correct. We want her recaptured, and we'll do a psych eval and put her away for good."

"That won't fly. You lost her once, and now she's murdered several men including Special Agent Brandon Sanderson of the FBI. We always get our man, or woman in this case. My officer's fiancée deserves to know that she was caught, faced trial, and will spend the remainder of her life in jail. Besides, even without this meeting, we have a head start on NCIS. We'll find her and arrest her before you ever have a chance. Dr. Quint has been the source for much of the evidence in this case. Someday you might consider adding someone with her skills to your staff."

Jill was downright embarrassed by Leticia's remarks. They were cringeworthy and probably could be attributed to a lack of sleep and the stress that the agent was under at the moment.

"Tell me about the evidence you have," Director Gomez requested.

Jill wondered what Leticia was going to say to that request. They had gone to the trouble of flying to San Diego. In her mind, that meant they should have a rational conversation about the case.

Jill was out of her element as she was just a consultant hired by the Sacramento Coroner's Office for one case. The fact that the case had blown up into something much bigger left her in uncertain territory. She had no personal stake in the case, and her personal safety had never been threatened, so she stayed silent.

"Jill, why don't you tell Director Gomez everything we learned about Amanda from the first death forward."

Okay, Jill thought, some direction going forward. She spent the next ten-plus minutes describing each crime scene and the evidence collected as well as the video of Amanda walking away from Agent Sanderson's house to the white truck. She also described the registered recreational vehicle that she towed behind it.

Once she finished, there was silence in the room as the two NCIS people focused on the new information. Once they finished absorbing what Jill described, she turned the tables on them and asked a few questions of her own.

"What did Amanda do that earned her a stay in the brig, and why have you been keeping this investigation a secret?"

The Director replied, "As you know, we trained an arsonist to be a munitions expert. A huge mistake on our part. She damaged the enemy, our property, and then, accidentally, one of her fellow soldiers. She's highly intelligent and has no family. She served a term in the brig and then was dishonorably discharged from the Navy. The first thing she did was violate her parole, and she hasn't been seen since. We've been looking for her since then."

"Why?" Jill asked. "Why put all this effort into one woman who didn't show up for parole? Surely you have bigger enemies to chase?"

Special Agent Lawrence stayed quiet, so Jill looked to Director Gomez for an answer and waited. He seemed to be weighing his thoughts on what to say.

"You never told the injured serviceman that she and the military deliberately caused his injuries and that you trained her and gave her the equipment to be as good as she is," SAC Ortiz guessed. "You're hiding a screw-up on the part of the military."

"No, Ma'am, we're just trying to capture a service member who has violated the laws of the military code of honor."

"I don't believe you. I guess we have nothing more to talk about. Her history will come out when she is taken into our custody, and at that time, you'll have to explain the grievous mistake you made in enlisting her. To be fair, arson is a rare trait among females, not something you can test for, but someone wasn't watching her behavior. You trained someone with an obsession with fire on how to be better at it. You gave her a variety of chemicals and methods she could continue to use as a civilian. I wonder how much damage and how many fires she has started thanks to her training here."

SAC Ortiz stood up and said to Jill, "You ready to head to the airport? We both have flights to catch home. We also have an ex-military member to apprehend."

They left the room, and the Director said, "Special Agent Lawrence, arrange for transport off the base for those women. They'll waste time trying to figure out how to be picked up. Stay close to them. We can always hope to take Amanda Moore into custody before they can."

"Sir, I don't think they'll go quietly. If you sent in a SEAL team to extract her, the FBI would cry foul, and we would be answering questions on Capitol Hill, especially since their agent was killed."

"Sadly, I think you might be right, Lawrence. I'm going to talk over this case with others, and then I'll let you know. You're dismissed."

Lawrence stood up, tamping down an urge to salute. This was a civilian-run agency, but military habits were hard to break. He left the building to find Agent Ortiz on the phone trying to arrange transport.

"Special Agent in Charge Ortiz, if you would let me, I'll arrange transport back to the airport. It can be tricky getting a ride-share car onto the base."

"Thank you, Special Agent Lawrence. I would appreciate that. Can we drop the titles? I'm Leticia, and this is Jill."

"Yes, Ma'am. I'm Jeff."

"Ma'am makes me feel old, just Leticia."

A car pulled up, and this time Lawrence got in the front, with Jill and Leticia in the back. They set off for the airport.

"I sure don't understand the military. It's far better to own up to your mistakes and move on than expending energy covering them up. She would have been a lot easier to find if you had requested the assistance of law enforcement years ago," Leticia said.

As the driver was wearing a military uniform, Leticia felt no need to hide her thoughts from the driver.

"We underestimated Amanda's intelligence and ability to stay hidden."

"Yeah, you did. Also, you lack law enforcement access to databases like the DMV."

"Can you tell me if at the time of her release from prison, she was taking any medications?" Jill asked.

"I don't have the information off the top of my head, but when I get back to my office, I'll look it up. Is there anything you're looking for specifically?"

"I've been talking to an ex-behavior analyst for the LAPD about the Burnt Widow. Specifically, what set her off at this time? She talked about treatment for obsessive-compulsive disorders, which is sometimes what arsonists are diagnosed with. I wondered if she recently ended psychotherapy or stopped taking medication."

"Those are good questions. I'll look them up when I review her file."

"Has she started fires at any military bases? I would think she would carry a certain amount of anger toward the military for her jail sentence."

"Yes, those started about the same time as the murders. Our bases have long perimeters, and it would be easy, out of sight of cameras, to approach one and start a fire. We have civilian firefighters on every base, so the blazes have been extinguished quickly. Still, in some instances, the fires have spread outside of the base, and that gets complicated."

Leticia decided she wanted to increase any guilt Special Agent Jeff Lawrence might feel by describing the upcoming funeral for FBI Agent Sanderson. It would be in three days and at a convention center in Sacramento. They expected upwards of ten-thousand law enforcement officers to show up, including the FBI Director. Most of the agents who died recently did so due to an illness related to the 9/11 tragedy in New York City and the

Pentagon. An agent hadn't been murdered by a criminal directly in the past twelve years.

After they got to the airport, Leticia and Jill went into the ladies' restroom.

"I was ready to start crying on the agent's behalf. I hadn't realized that FBI agents are rarely shot in the line of duty. This is going to be such a sad event. I also realize you were discussing it to lay more guilt on the Special Agent."

"Yes, you're right on all accounts."

The three of them went their separate ways, and Jeff didn't wait around for Jill once he exited the plane after it landed. Jill was late getting back to Nathan's house that night and just wanted to head for bed.

CHAPTER 30

*A*manda Moore had a list of all the military bases in California. On her bucket list was torching each of the twenty-seven bases. So far, she had started fires at five bases in Northern California, but unfortunately, none of them raged out-of-control. As she moved south, she planned to continue lighting fires. The problem was the eastern side of the state. There were bases in fairly remote areas that would take her a long time to reach. Maybe she would go after those bases last. She could sweep south and then head to the eastern side of the state when she was finished in San Diego.

In the back of her head, she was feeling pressure for the first time that law enforcement was getting close. She tensed whenever she saw a cop. Were they coming for her? Should she change the paint of her truck, or ditch it? Were they on to her recreational vehicle?

Also, she wanted to get better with the wildfires she was starting at the bases. She would love to see a brushfire get out of control and wipe out an entire base. She could buy a flame thrower, but she would have to stay in one area for several days waiting for it to arrive. She looked for stores that sold them, and there were a few around Sacramento. She planned to stop and buy one the next day. She could run with a flame thrower along the fence protecting the perimeter of any base and start a much larger fire that spread faster if she had a little mechanical help from such a gadget.

She also wanted to stop at a large library to use their internet to locate the two women at the press conference who had been talking about her work. She planned to burn their properties down, hopefully with them inside their houses. First, she needed to find out where they lived and scope out their properties. Once she knew that, she would plan her attack and decide where to go next. She paid the fee to park her recreational vehicle at a campground, unhitched her pick-up truck, and went out to handle things.

First, she investigated getting the truck painted. She checked with several places, and she would be without her vehicle for two to three days. She could rent a car in the interim to continue her work. She didn't want to be on record for using a credit card at the moment as it was traceable. She inquired as to whether she could drive one of the cars from the rental shop while they had her truck in the paint shop. They agreed, which pleased her as she could use it to reach a military base or two in the area. She left the truck in the paint shop and next traveled to an industrial supply company to purchase the flame thrower. Next, she visited the library to look up the home addresses of Special Agent in Charge Leticia Ortiz and Dr. Jill Quint. She wanted to leave no evidence of her plans on the computer in her RV.

She was frustrated when she couldn't locate the address of either woman after an hour of searching. She found a biography about the agent, and it mentioned a husband and kids. She looked for property in the husband's name and scored a house in San Francisco. It was a dangerous place to try to burn down as there were people everywhere, and it would be hard not to be caught. She then went looking at the history of property ownership of Dr.

Quint. She had owned a property in Sacramento, then in a small city that Amanda looked up. It was called the Palisades Valley, and she sold a property there about a year ago, then purchased a property in Kern County farther to the south. She looked up that property on Google Earth and decided it was a decoy. It had a shack on it and was in the middle of nowhere. This was not the house of a physician, even if she was a forensic pathologist. Amanda looked a little longer and saw that Jill Quint sold the property to a corporation. She researched the corporation but couldn't find anything on it. She had time on her hands, so she would journey to San Francisco and to the Palisades Valley to see what her opportunities were.

She researched where she might find some roads in the area that weren't well-traveled. She needed to try her flame thrower against a deserted road. She just wanted to make sure she understood the settings of the model she bought. For once, her goal was not to start a fire but just to test her equipment. Like a good soldier, she smiled to herself. She found exactly what she was looking for and then headed back to her campsite. She needed to get work done if she wanted to pay for things like the paint job and the flame thrower.

The next day, she headed to San Francisco to look at the agent's house. She parked on the street and used binoculars to get an idea of where exterior building cameras were on the street. Like so many houses in San Francisco, there wasn't much distance between houses. If she managed to light the agent's house on fire, it would likely take out one or both of her neighbors' houses. Her best bet was to wait until dark and scale one of the side yard fences. She could get a nice fire going in the back of the house, delaying discovery and increasing destruction. It appeared that the bedrooms were on the second level, and she had no way to pump in carbon monoxide like she did with the other agent's house. She studied the front door and wondered if she could put a steel pipe between the door latch and the doorframe to prevent the door from being opened for the family to escape. The trouble with that idea was she could see a porch camera that would likely alert the family to her work. She would have to do the pipe idea just before she ran away from the property. Oh well, the agent and her family would very likely escape with their lives through the first-floor windows. With a plan in her head, she drove toward the Palisades Valley.

Two hours later, she slowed her car to look at the property that Dr. Jill Quint once owned. There was a sign that said Quixotic Winery. She continued a mile beyond the driveway to the house and pulled off the road. She had filmed the property as she slowly drove by. She hadn't noticed any cameras beyond those at the front gate, which was closed. She looked up the name of the winery and smiled when she read the owner's bio.

It was Dr. Jill Quint in the flesh. She must be trying to hide her property ownership through the corporation. Amanda supposed that Jill could have sold just the house but kept the vineyard and the buildings that housed wine production. Maybe Amanda would tell Jill Quint just before she killed her that she should have fixed her website. She had a chuckle at that thought.

It was time to go home and catch some sleep. She had a lot of work planned for that night. She wanted to start fires on three bases and at two houses. It would take her all night to achieve her goal. Tomorrow she would return the car, pick up her truck, and then head south about one-hundred miles and lay low at a rarely used campground. Amanda planned to read all the news reports and privately crow at the destruction she would wield. Depending on her outcomes with the three base fires, she would continue her path of destruction south. On that pleasant thought, she fell asleep.

Her alarm woke her several hours later. Amanda had learned the trick of sleeping at will when she served in the military. She prepared a big dinner accompanied by a caffeine-rich sports drink. Her plan was to strike the three military bases before midnight before heading into San Francisco to take care of the agent. Her final assignment of the night was Jill Quint's house, which she would strike about three in the morning by her calculation. She dressed in all black and had grease paint to use once she reached her first location. She'd put a temporary black rinse on her hair, covered it with a ball cap, and was wearing gloves. It was still hot in the evening, but she kept the car's air-conditioning on so she could wear a long sleeve shirt. When she arrived at her first target, an airfield devoted to the Coast Guard, she decided to cross that base off her list as it was so small and exposed. She next had on her list an Air Force base north of Sacramento and one to the south. The one to the north was surrounded by dry brush, and she couldn't wait to let her flame thrower go to work on that base.

It had miles of deserted fencing that called to her. She loved that it was so dark and deserted here. The initial smoke from the fire wouldn't show for a while. She would get a nice spread of the fire before the base staff noticed it. Also, there was a twenty MPH wind that she cheered about as it pushed the flames toward the base. She found the deserted road she was looking for and parked the car and gathered her equipment. She had hoped to run along the fence line, but she could see that the idea wouldn't work as the ground was uneven, and the last thing she wanted to do was trip. Instead, she walked the fence line to the right of her vehicle, figuring she'd cover about two-hundred yards on both sides of her against the fence line. She turned the flame thrower on and torched the area as fast as she could walk while keeping her balance. She'd thought of getting night vision goggles, but the flame would have blinded her night vision.

The most beautiful fire was roaring. She could feel its power and the sound of its roar. She was mesmerized watching the flames dance across the field. In the distance, she thought she heard sirens, which surprised her. She thought it would take at least another five minutes before she heard the first siren. Maybe the base had aerial surveillance from a landing plane, or a drone had caught sight of the flames. She hopped into the car and moved toward the main road with just her parking lights on. She hit the main road and turned away from this base and on to the next.

When Amanda arrived at the next Air Force base, she was dismayed to see they had a large nighttime operation in progress, or so it looked to her. Runway lights were on, and sitting where she was in the car, she could see the lights shining on her. She would have to circle back to this base at a later date.

At this time of the night, it would take less than an hour to reach the agent's house in San Francisco. She had four one-gallon jugs of isopropyl alcohol, which was her accelerant of choice. She cruised the agent's street with the lights off several times. There was no activity. She parked the car and quickly grabbed her bag of accelerants and a tiny fuse she planned to light just before she hopped into her car to make an escape. She pulled herself over the fence carrying the tools of fire. In under five minutes, she had splashed the isopropyl alcohol against the house, outlining its shape in the backyard. She soaked her fuse and unwound the cord just before she set a match to it and ran for her car. Just as she was sliding into the car, she could hear sirens close by. She didn't know whether they were fire trucks, ambulances, or police vehicles. She did know she'd better get out of there fast. It wouldn't do to be seen leaving a burning house in a hurry. She made random turns on the streets of San Francisco, getting away from the agent's house. After five minutes, she punched the button on her phone's GPS to direct her to the city of Palisades Valley.

Amanda felt pretty good about herself having lit two spectacular fires that night. She was hoping for a third when she struck Dr. Jill Quint's house.

CHAPTER 31

*J*ill was nestled in Nathan's arms when she heard her phone ringing. She opened it and saw the caller, and punched the button to connect. She got out of bed, trying not to jostle Nathan as she did so. Seconds later, she was in the hallway heading for the kitchen.

"Hello."

"Hi Jill, it's Leticia. The Burnt Widow is having a busy night. First, there was a fire at an Air Force base in Yuba County, and then an attempt was made on my house. She spread accelerant around the back of my house and then tossed a match. I think your house might be next tonight."

"Oh, no! Did you suffer a lot of damage to your house? Do you have video surveillance of your house that captures the Burnt Widow?"

"Actually, don't tell my neighbors, but we had cameras set up on their house focused on my house. The motion detector software sent me an alert, and I, in turn, called the fire department. We're fortunate; not much damage was done. A good part of the accelerant didn't have a chance to burn. You want to know the scary thing?"

"What did she do?"

"She took some kind of metal spike and taped it with duct tape inside the latch of my front door. If my family had actually been inside, the rear exit would have been blocked by fire, and the front exit had the metal spike preventing the door from opening inward. My husband says he would have had us out quickly as he would've taken the hinges off the door and opened it from the other side. Still, this woman is scary. The house is in my husband's name, and if you Google him, you'll find pictures of our kids. I'm sure the woman knew that and didn't care that she might be killing two children."

"Wow, she's quite evil. So you're thinking I'm next because she's picking off the people that were at the press conference?"

"Yes. You're the third piece of the triangle here, so you have a bulls-eye on your back. If I were you, I would alert your fire department to be ready. I would also call your sheriff and put him on alert, and I would pull your security cameras up and watch them. It might take her ninety minutes to get from my place to yours at this time of night. You have another thirty minutes before she arrives."

"Thanks for the heads-up, Leticia. I'm going to get dressed and head over to my house. Hopefully, I'll be there before her."

"Jill, I would advise that you stay away from your property. She is very dangerous, and you do not want to go up in flames along with your house." Jill shuddered, thinking about her fear of fire. Would she even have the nerve to face off with the Burnt Widow? What if she was holding a torch or something?

"I'll take Nathan with me. With all the cameras on my property, we should be able to take her on."

"Jill, call your sheriff. You need help."

"I don't want to scare her away. If she sees the lights of a police car, we'll likely lose our best chance to capture her."

"Jill, I'm going to call your sheriff in a moment. An officer can park his vehicle in your garage, so it's out of sight. If she shows up with a flame thrower, none of your martial arts training will serve you well. She'll have a far greater reach that you can't overcome."

"You have a point. I've got to hang up now to get dressed and out the door and in position before she arrives. I'll call you later."

Rather than call dispatch, Jill called Officer Emma Davis. She often worked the night shift, was really good with a rifle, and had saved Jill's life multiple times. She explained what was going on with her latest investigative case. Emma estimated she would be at Jill's house in fifteen minutes. Jill gave her the passcode to park inside the garage.

"Having a police car parked inside the garage when a house is on fire is probably a bad idea," Emma replied.

"I don't have another building to hide your car inside."

"It's your lucky night. I'm driving an unmarked vehicle as my patrol car is in for maintenance. I'll park it in front of your garage but take the government plates off."

"That will work. I'm going to park down the road and walk to my house with Nathan. We've got to get going if we're to beat the arrival of the Burnt Widow."

With that, Jill walked into the bedroom, turning the lights on, and woke Nathan up.

"Special Agent in Charge Ortiz believes that the arsonist is on her way to my house. I have Deputy Emma Davis on her way there now. We need to leave as soon as we get some clothes on."

Nathan didn't ask any questions. He just got dressed. Once they were in her car and on the way, she told him about the fire at Leticia's house. She also described her plan for protecting her property and capturing the arsonist. He couldn't think of a better plan.

Jill pulled into a convenience store parking lot about half a mile from her house. Jill saw lights approaching on the road and hoped it was not the Burnt Widow. She released her breath when she saw Emma's unmarked police car.

They moved over to Emma's car, and she pulled out onto the road and toward Jill's vineyard.

"I never know whether to love or hate the phone calls I get from you, Jill Quint," Emma said. "You're usually in some kind of bad trouble, but you make my shift go much faster, and I get a rush of adrenaline trying to arrest whoever's trying to kill you."

"Personally, I love having you on my side. You're really good with a gun and cool under fire. That's the kind of help I need when I'm facing down a crazy criminal."

"Gee, what am I, chopped liver?" asked Nathan.

"Nathan, the problem with you and me is we're good at those martial arts moves, but we're not faster than a speeding bullet, which is where Emma comes in."

The tension in the cruiser was thick. Emma drove by Jill's property, but they saw no cars or trucks on the road or parked in a certain radius around Jill's house. They drove back to her house, and she used a remote to open the gate and close it again as soon as they were through. If the arsonist got close enough to the vehicle and looked in the windows, she would see that it was a police car. Jill tried to talk the officer into parking it inside her garage, but Emma was adamant that she needed to keep the car safe if the fire did start.

In the end, Jill had her park the car against the side of her barn that couldn't be seen from the road. The car was in a safe spot yet wouldn't get damaged if Jill's house caught fire.

Jill looked at her watch and said, "If she was coming straight here from Leticia's house, she should be here in about ten minutes. Where should we hide?"

"I would argue between the house and the vineyard. Most of your criminals seem to think they can walk to your vineyard and attack the house. If we lay in wait in the dark, we should get a warning of when the Burnt Widow enters the property, and that will clue us in to which path she's taking," Nathan said.

"I wonder how she found me. I went to all the trouble of transferring ownership of the winery to a corporation, and yet she still connected it to me."

"You don't know that. Maybe she's not coming here at all. Maybe we're sitting outside in the dark for nothing," Nathan suggested.

Emma was typing something on her phone. She would need backup quickly if things went south here. Maybe she had the other patrol car parked in the same lot as Jill's car. The deputy looked up from her phone and said, "You have your picture and name on your winery website. You may have gone through the trouble of transferring your property to a corporation, but you forgot to fix your website."

"Darn, I thought I was so smart protecting my property."

Jill heard the unmistakable sounds of a car approaching on the road. She whispered to Emma and Nathan, "Maybe this is her."

The three of them watched and said almost in unison, "It's the Burnt Widow." What other explanation was there for the car slowing as it passed Jill's property with its lights off at three in the morning? If it was an intoxicated driver, they would've hit a tree by now. The car continued past the vineyard entrance, and they heard it pull over. A car door opened, and then they heard a second sound.

Jill looked at Nathan and whispered, "What's that sound?"

"I think she was getting something out of the trunk."

Emma was talking quietly on her police radio. Jill wished she had thought to bring her night-vision goggles with her. If the Burnt Widow had them, she would see them much sooner than they would see her. That was a scary proposition as the arsonist could torch them before they had a chance to take cover. She had sweat rolling off of her at the thought of dying in a flame.

"We have a second patrol car, a fire truck, and an ambulance in the lot where we left your car. I have my body camera on so they can see and hear what's going on."

"We think she got something out of the trunk."

"Doesn't she use accelerants at most of her arson scenes? It would make sense that she would drive with them in her trunk. Anyone looking at the back seat of her car would be suspicious if she was carrying several gas containers."

"Isopropyl alcohol containers," Jill whispered.

"Iso what?" Emma asked.

Jill described what she had done to the victims as well as at Agent Ortiz's house.

They were quiet and listened for any sounds.

They thought they heard the sound of a boot on dry soil. The three of them were crouched in a vine row farthest from the road. Jill caught movement and tapped the arms of Emma and Nathan to point out where she was.

Jill was milliseconds away from gasping out loud at what the woman was carrying in her hands. She thought she had seen pictures of it—it was a flame thrower. She almost lost it right there, she was so angry at the thought that this woman was going to burn her house down.

She whispered to Nathan, "I'm going after that arsonist. I'm not going to let her torch everything I love and have worked for on this vineyard. I'm going to turn the vineyard's bright lights on, and we'll go from there."

Deputy Davis listened and shook her head in agreement. "Turn your lights on and see what she does next. Does she continue toward the house, or is she freaked out by the security lights and so she stops advancing on your house?"

Jill nodded, liking the deputy's idea. Jill did a silent count while holding her phone, ready to swipe the app that controlled her security system. They all momentarily shut their eyes, knowing about the blinding light coming. When they were able to see under the bright lights, they noted that the invader was holding night vision goggles in one hand. She would be blind for a few moments as bright lights are especially painful when viewed through night-vision lenses.

Jill and Nathan sprang to a sprint to reach the perpetrator. Emma, loaded down with a bulletproof vest and equipment belt, walked speedily toward the three people grappling on the ground. She moved the flame thrower away from the arsonist and pulled her handcuffs off her toolbelt. In short order, Nathan had the woman's hands behind her back as she was face down on the dirt. Jill could see flashing lights moving toward the house. Emma's backup was here.

"Let me go! It's dark out, and I accidentally wandered onto this property. I've done nothing wrong, and you must release me."

Jill shined her cell phone light at the woman they had captured. It was an older Amanda Moore, but she smiled that they had trapped their arsonist.

"Hello Amanda Moore, or are you more used to the name Allison Montgomery? Local law enforcement and the FBI have been looking for you. As I'm sure you know, I'm Dr. Jill Quint. I'm a pathologist who found your DNA at all of the crime scenes where you murdered male dates."

"I don't know what you're talking about, and I don't know who Amanda Moore is."

Jill said to the two sheriff's deputies, "If you want to put her in your jail, there are several people who plan to prosecute her. She's wanted for the murder of FBI Special Agent Brandon Sanderson. She's wanted by the state fire marshal for starting brushfires. She's likely started fires in or near military bases, so they may want to interview her too. Why don't we all head for the sheriff's station? I'll call Special Agent in Charge Ortiz and see about getting an FBI team here to interview her."

Jill made a call to Ortiz, cheering on the fact that they had the Burnt Widow in custody. Leticia was on her way to the Palisades Valley. Jill also called Special Agent Lawrence and woke him up.

"We just took Amanda Moore into custody after she was clearly planning on burning my house down."

"Where is she now?"

"On her way to the jail under the custody of the Palisades Valley Sheriff. Special Agent Ortiz is on her way. Here's the address of the sheriff's station."

EPILOGUE

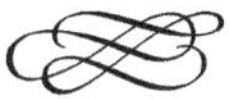

Jill was dressed in a slim, severe black dress with pearls at her neck. Her hair was pulled back in a tight bun, and she looked graceful on three-inch heels. At her side, Nathan was handsome in a dark suit, white shirt, and gray tie. They were on their way inside Arco Arena for the funeral of Agent Sanderson.

His casket arrived behind a motorcycle escort of CHP officers. The hearse drove under a large American flag suspended from two hook and ladder fire trucks. From across the nation, law enforcement officers arrived to pay tribute to a lone FBI agent they hadn't known except as a brother in arms. A limousine carrying Brandon's fiancée, Leticia, and the FBI Director followed the hearse. There was silence as Brandon's flag-draped casket was removed from the vehicle, and then eight pallbearers wearing FBI jackets moved the casket to its designated spot in the arena. There were pictures of the agent at various times in his career, and the last one was his engagement picture, Jill guessed.

The service started with a prayer, and then the FBI Director made his opening remarks. Music was played as they moved between speakers who started with scriptures and moved on to stories about his life. Brandon's fiancée didn't speak, and Jill couldn't blame her. It was an emotionally exhausting day. Jill discussed the case she worked with the agent and the fact that it resulted in his death. She also tried to lighten the room, talking about her fear of fire and how the agent talked her through it. After more speakers, the casket was carried by the pallbearers back to the hearse, and many cars lined up to form a long funeral cortege to the cemetery. Once there, a twenty-one gun salute was followed by folding the flag for Brandon's fiancée. The graveside service ended with bagpipes playing "Amazing Grace."

Jill had managed to barely hold it together throughout the service, but when the bagpipes played their sorrowful music, she lost it and had rivulets of tears running down her face. Nathan passed her tissues and hugged her back to his car. They got inside and waited while the traffic began to clear.

"That was about the saddest funeral I've ever been to," Nathan said.

"I warned you, and thanks for taking a day off work to accompany me here. I knew it was going to be an emotional day made all the worse by the symbols of a law enforcement funeral."

"I guess you've attended a few over the years in your prior role as a medical examiner."

"Actually, no. This is the first and hopefully the last I'll ever attend."

"It really serves to remind you when you see someone as young as Brandon Sanderson that life is short.

They were quiet during the drive home to the Palisades Valley, each lost in their own thoughts. They entered the gates of her vineyard to be greeted by Trixie. They went inside, and Jill kicked off her shoes and sat leaning against Nathan, sipping wine from a bottle he opened.

"Rest in peace, Agent Sanderson," Jill said, clinking her wine glass to Nathan's as they watched the breeze keep a huge leaf aloft and dancing across her vineyard.

The End

ALSO BY ALEC PECHE

Jill Quint, MD Forensic Pathologist Series

Time's Up (prequel short story)

Vials

Chocolate Diamonds

A Breck Death

Death On A Green

A Taxing Death

Murder At The Podium

Castle Killing

Crescent City Murder

Sicilian Murder

Opus Murder

Forensic Murder

Return to the Scene of the Crime (short story)

Embers of Murder

Ashes to Murder

Mint Death

Damian Green Series

Red Rock Island

Willow Glen Heist

The Girl From Diana Park

Evergreen Valley Murder

Long Delayed Justice

Michelle Watson Series

Now You Don't See Me

Where Did She Go?

How Did She Get There?

<u>Dog Humor</u>

Eat, Play, Poop: Letters to my parents from camp

<u>New Urban Fantasy Series - Stephanie Jones</u>

The Awakening at Lake Tahoe (short story)

Witch's Medicine (2024)

ABOUT THE AUTHOR

I reside in Northern California with my rescue dog and cat. I love to travel, play sports, read, and drink wine and beer. I enjoy the diversity of the world and I'm always watching people and events for story ideas. All of my stories are generated by my imagination, I don't use AI to write books.

If you would like to sign up for my bi-weekly blog and announcement of new books, please follow this link: https://www.AlecPecheBooks.com

While you're waiting for the next story, if you would be so kind as to leave a review for this book, that would be great. I appreciate all the feedback and support. Reviews buoy my spirits and stoke the fires of creativity.

Readers that sign up for my blog receive a free prequel novelette for the Jill Quint Series.